SAVING HISTORY

Also by Fanny Howe

Poetry

Prose

SAVING HISTORY

FANNY HOWE

SUN & MOON CLASSICS: 27

LOS ANGELES, CALIFORNIA

SUN &
MOON

CLASSICS

27

Sun & Moon Press
A Program of
The Contemporary Arts Council Project, Inc.
a non-profit corporation
6026 Wilshire Boulevard, Los Angeles, CA 90036

First published in paperback in 1993 by Sun & Moon Press

10 9 8 7 6 5 4 3 2 1
FIRST EDITION

Portions of this book have appeared in
United Artists, Sulfur, Avec, and
Cradle and All (edited by Laura Chester).

This book was made possible, in part, through a grant from the Cultural Affairs
Department, City of Los Angeles, from the National Endowment for the Arts,
and through contributions to the Contemporary Arts Educational Project, Inc.,
a non-profit corporation.

Cover photograph: Colleen McCallion
Reproduced by permission of the artist
Design: Katie Messborn
Typography: Jim Cook

LIBRARY OF CONGRESS CATALOGING IN PUBLICATION DATA
Fanny Howe (1940)
Saving History
p. cm — (Sun & Moon Classics: 27)
ISBN: 1-55713-100-7
I. Title. II. Series.
811'.54—dc19
CIP 90-50333

Printed in the United States of America

For Quincy Howe, Jr.

This universe is a machine for effecting the salvation of those who consent to it.

—SIMONE WEIL

One

Unable to rest because unable to know.

If Christ doesn't rise in two hours, then God has forsaken us all. The whitening of the east spreads over the west. Mourning doves warble.

Morning men are raving on the beach, of alcohol and some mental derangement associated with loss.

He told me all love doesn't end in tragedy. But he admitted that this was only HIS experience.

He had had, he told me, many happy love experiences. Of course they were all in the past tense. . . .

He had painted his walls black, and the windows were always sealed by green blinds. You could see nothing, except a small ring of light around votive candles. It was a building filled with young prostitutes, overlooking a miserable avenue in the south end of town. He had some political posters hung on walls, but only after your eyes grew accustomed to the light could you actually read the words: SOLEDAD, WATTS, UP THE IRA. . . .

Her skin did not respond to touches lacking in love. The first thing you really know is the touch of love. So why did she return again to his black bedclothes, to the pressure of his body on hers? She did not believe in choice, because she misapprehended facts. They had eluded her since childhood. Anything that had a weight, measurement and number—a correct answer—became blurry as the face of an enemy. She averted her gaze from facts. She lived impressionistically, with the kind of awe that makes you egalitarian. She didn't love him either, not at first, not until it was clear that they were stuck together in the tragedy of consequence.

In that city there was none of the convulsive unity you find in the great cities of this century—Paris, New York. There was none of that sense of the violent and the tender occurring simultaneously, as they might on a farm or a plantation. No, each element of expression was segregated from the other. It was a divided city, provincial and proud, dominated by the ethics of Protestants. In this city she developed her fear of institutions, a fear that was neurotic, if colorful. It led her to the usual ironies—a sentence of time spent enclosed in brick. But first she had to succumb to being fueled by this man who did not love her and never would. He would claim her, insult her, beat her, he would lie to himself and others about her, he would conjure her into alien forms—hostile and subversive— after he had married her and made her pregnant more than once. And she would collaborate, for reasons unknown. Both did what they did for reasons unknown to them (the one liberating aspect to the arrangement), and both suffered equally though suffering can't be measured or numbered, and either you do, or you don't suffer.

Outside the sheep of snow lay down along the curbs. I have heard a book roar with a snowstorm inside it. People froze between the pages. Beasts nuzzled their own teats.

I experience my abilities to think and imagine as actual geographies, specters. But I know that consciousness does not dwell in me, but I dwell in it.

Everyone's terror weighs the same. The critical issue is how to release it from its venue—to what we call Liberty: whether by standing on the ocean-swept deck obedient but in prayer. Or whether by setting off bombs. To liberate the terror. And vacate the premises where terror laps like an unwanted animal at a pool of water. Then to live with a little space in oneself, to brush it and sweep it and wash it with tears. And never to let terror enter again, never.

He said Orpheus is everything. He made a religion of language, a paradise of words. A French nurse had named him Dumas when she found out he was "Hugo" and he was only a baby. He said this act of nominal determinism made him the poet he believed himself to be, and he was. How could he not be when he was so arbitrarily named? "I was named and so I name."

His voice was the voice of The End.

He made the choice. She was submissive.

For reasons unknown, they fixed on each other, fascinated, and directed all discourse, one to the other, quarreling but unwilling to let go, whether by phone or by face or by mail. Hugo was the color of sanded cedar, he came from the Seychelles originally, then Tanzania (where he witnessed slaughter and was tortured) and Ibiza. His mother came from Punjab, his father was a priest. He was in the import business, but it continually failed him, and so he was a voracious reader of literature about struggle.

We don't care about her name yet because she has the advantage of the I.

I couldn't say it was love, but I don't think a woman can love a man unless it's her father or her son. I could say, though, that it was one interior life enclosing the other's, and one intelligence devouring the other's, and the way fate works when it wants to change society.

Fate eats. God announces itself as affliction, as a pain that is gruesome. God doesn't eat, but wounds. You have to know this in order to live.

When people decided to mix inventions into the real things—cement in water, steel pipes in earth, tiles under fields—they were only a few steps away from putting nails into hands, people into ovens, needles into arms.

I identify with the women standing back and watching the crucifixion drama, because I know how easy it is to become a participant in cruelty. And once that has happened, what's left for you? Better to stand aside.

He couldn't care for anyone but himself, because the givens of his personality were overwhelming. He was a person who only slept three hours out of every twenty-four. His mind raced, always had. His reading was voracious, scattered, but he put all the information together—from no matter what sources—into a unifying, and credible theory. He was drawn to criminals and prostitutes. He didn't want to be one with them, but watched them with a dull pain in his temples. It was their unenlightenment that plagued him, interested him, an absence of self-consciousness that was synonymous with no-law. He lacked a superego himself (or conscience) while he sometimes lay prone in prayer to Allah. It was his cowardice that finally acted in place of a conscience. He was really scared of being discovered and labeled.

I don't know this man but I suffer for him. How? I live out his drama, mentally, trying to imagine the way it felt to be him. I hope that in this imaginative action, some of his pain will revert to me. If I don't do this, who else will?

It was her assignment for a few years to receive his blows and his cruel words. When it was no longer her assignment, and servitude was turning into slavery, she left, and he followed, making brutal and realizable threats on her life. They both, this way, entered a life of detachment, as in antisocial.

To kill and destroy in order to make room for business and technology is to have reached the conclusion that what a person makes has more value than the person.

We have only ourselves—compositional under misty givens—to blame. And only other human hands can transmit the tenderness we require. I can live without almost anything except love. The sexual frenzy of the exiting spirit is an expression of this poverty of desire.

All women are prostitutes, he insisted. Wives are variations on that theme of utility. The wedding ring was a link in a human chain, hand to hand to hand, around the globe. The sign of the master-whore engagement was that gold band on a hand. He pointed out the flounciness of females on the streets, their pathetic embellishment of their bodies. Men embellish their egos, he said. Women embellish their flesh. They can't help being beautiful of course, he conceded. And together they scrutinized the females passing, experiencing the wounds of appreciation at the faces they saw. But then he would accuse her of decadence, when she noted beauty on her own. It was hard to keep up with his varying judgements, always contradicting themselves from day to day. She was too sensitive to him, to all inflections of judgement in fact. Yet they agreed on books, movies, plays, politics; their opinions mirrored each other, no matter how wild and speculative they were. Something twinned in the way they both thought feelingly; their brains were receivers and purveyors of emotions and they organized their thoughts into streams of near-ecstatic perceptions. While most people experienced their brains as dry factories of ideas, and memories, they did not.

The poetics of speech—especially angry speech—was their folie à deux.

He bought her a thick gold band encrusted with rhinestones. It had an antique look, she lost it, and he had to buy her two other rings before their day was over. I want to understand why a woman would try so hard to please a man who was cold and unkind. What's the deal? All people seek great difficulty, no doubt about that; they seek and even create the situation which will be insurmountably problematic. It would be a strange person who did not know that suffering is a way to stay alive.

Having learned the heavy stresses and the light—between subjugation and servitude—I will stand behind my actions, without a jot of remorse.

He smashed his fist into her face, as it lay on a pillow, and a geyser of warm blood rushed from her nostrils, she thought she was blind. At the hospital they diagnosed a broken nose, she had two black eyes for several days, and wore dark glasses. He was repentant, stunned, saddened by his unexpected bash. She forgave but couldn't forget what he had done. She flinched automatically when he leaned over her to turn off the light.

He anyway returned to his anger soon after, and directed it again at her. Words, words, poisoned words, about her background, her privilege (at not having been tortured as a child, at not losing her family to war), her inability to understand what it was like to be him. They lived under trees—swinging beech and elm trees—by then, in a rundown section on the margin of the city, a section that had once been elegant and summery. Rain ran lines down the dusty windowpanes. Her babies pressed their pink lips against her nipples and drank with their eyes raised to see her face. Their hands waved vaguely, they were "Irish twins" born within a year of each other, and sometimes by chance their fingers linked, as if they were members of the same body.

She was his mother, in the sense that she was the mother he owned. Mother? What, in fact, is a mother? It is the description of a person who has given birth. They say you only have one mother, but men who marry women who then give birth have two mothers. Equally, he was her second father, being the father whom she owned through the arrangement of their physical relations. Her father. So sex has astounding consequences, conferring profound titles on those involved.

This was the center of both of their lives: the pit heart, the fall point, the cemetery at the center of all that is given. Sparrows had seeds, worms, and water, and they had food stamps, greens, and wine. Everything they had, though, was shoved to the side to accommodate the heavy presence of his past. Clock, phone, radio, rain.

His hand would lift like a slide rule, tilted, his lips narrowed, when he wanted to hit her but didn't. He was utterly lacking the tenderness of a person who has felt safe in the beginning (his beginnings were wretched and insulting, his belly and back a story of scars), but he was not innately violent. It was alcohol that incinerated the patience that was a good characteristic of his. Without that ability to stand in a line for a long time, or to sit in a waiting room quietly, reading, his essence was sunk. He was, with wine in him, restless, raging.

She lay in bed a lot, after work, with the babies on either side, sipping a can of Champale, watching t.v. When she heard his tread, her mouth grew parched. Most times he would come in and only abuse her verbally. But once he pulled her roughly away from the babies, dragged her down the hall, and stabbed at her stiff torso with his phallus. He knew she only loved her children, he felt neglected and abandoned. She dreamed he murdered her double and buried the body in a baggie out in the yard, and she covered for him. By "dream" I mean she entered into her true story, sleeping.

He was verbally flashy, and mentally quick as anyone, he could have been a money-maker except he was so inconsistent, and so quick to hate. He said things like, "If you aren't a money-maker in one of the American states, you are as good as wastepaper. You have to fight to be multi-rich or lie down, dirt poor. There's nowhere to be comfortable between. Why do I have to feel so anxious about money? What is it? Numbers!"

Even their shared interests did not "hold them together" but, instead, did the opposite. When he took the ferry to the city past the Statue of Liberty three days a week, sitting on wooden benches with persons on the flat barge rolling over the water—

The blueing of the east has begun. One bird shows frantic pleasure in this fact. Where are the bodies of fallen sparrows? There are so many of them lined up on wires, posted on rooftops, nestled in trees, you'd think their bodies—

The central question for Hugo: Was violence voluntary or a compulsion? In other words, did he make a choice to strike out or was he chosen? And what might happen to him now?

As they grew, the kids (a girl and a girl) kept each other busy under tables and on jolly swings where they bounced side by side, hanging from the doorjamb facing both hall and kitchen. As toddlers, they both loved vanilla yogurt, flan, and Gerber's mixed fruits. Only one ate meat, which the littler one declined with a grimace.

Gray firmament, predawn, I am distanced from others and self, milking unending desire for union with the end of alone. The two stars that travel over the telephone wires. . . . The placement of the moon above the chimney. . . . Now I am conscious of such repetition and distance as being salves of the psyche.

Why do women let an old man dominate their fortunes? Why do the children vote for fathers instead of brothers? Why do men have this power over women and children? The erotic swelling . . . the necessity of birthing . . . must these cause such abject behavior that the earth itself is being shaken from its axis by the spill of weapons?

One night he whammed and slammed her, knocking her right down the stone steps in front of their house. Then he launched off into the city, his face as twisted as a gargoyle on a cathedral wall. She made her way inside and stuffed clothes into a trash bag, dragged the children out into the cold, and lay them to sleep on the bag in the rear section of the car.

Snow spackled the windshield when she finally sped over the highway that night. She had a destination. It was Quebec, the very name of which elicits a rapture from her each time she hears it. The roads were at first prone and sad and then leaping and dangerous. All French references were darkened by the hour. The girls snored on the backseat. Even that far north she glanced in the rearview mirror to see if he was following. Snow was the music to which she rhymed the lyrics of her thoughts under her fractured nose and blue cheeks.

Stood up, square lights, the children and I will enter mono-
lithic cities together, but I will be too small to save them
from the dangers there. O Carmelite poets, come to my rescue! Teresa, San Juan de la Cruz, Sor Juana. . . . Dawn
flooded the northern whites with a blue beam. It did strange
things to the ice crossing lakes. Still the snow dreamed its
way down to ground, and she had to move slowly, unsteadily,
towards a plate of pancakes, maple syrup, and hot coffee.

Erotic thoughts kept her going. Nests give birth to birds, we
don't know where they die. But the little bloodfilled fist
swells in a swaddling of twigs, hidden among the leaves, and
finally splits its pink beak open to the sun. I am horrored by
necessity: by the squeezing clam, the bubbles of suck in the
sand, and by the automatism of the bird's motions. I am horrored by the bulge of violence, so built into all living systems.
But the milk that pricks and dribbles from my nipples is the
same milk that nurtures the violent arts. And the milk of my
groin is the same . . . .

She knew he would find her. There is an intuitive map drawn
on the wall of a compulsive person. This was the map he followed and which invariably led him to her. It always worked
that way between them, that he would arrive just when she
was beginning to work at a project of her own, that he would
call, just when someone he hated had arrived, that he would
find her talking to someone he considered an enemy. Now
she knew he would trail through the backest woods of all and
find her and the children. Sometimes she understood that
this was not a conscious plan for him, and that he was surprised by what he stumbled on. It was as if he was receiving
signals from somewhere else, ones so subtle that he himself

lived unconscious of them even as he followed them. He would, she realized, want to locate her, but nonetheless he would experience his finding her as a semi-surprise. He would think he was just heading up to Quebec on a whim, or a business venture. And there she would be, walking the sweet streets of Quebec City! He would turn the corner and there she would be! Behind her in a plate glass window would be a display of rubber phalluses, which she didn't want the kids to see. And between them would be the icy wind of marriage. Breath-unifying. Tragic marriage!

Ecstasy reversed: where in ecstasy there is largeness, liquidity, joy, space, confidence and union—now in the case of such an encounter, there is a squeezed feeling, dryness, terror, confinement, loneliness and loss of hope. Yet there was something of one in the other. It was the sense of INEVITABIL-ITY. They had that in common.

The wounded boy is the mean man. Trouble is, he's got both muscles and mind. I get so flattened by harsh verbiage that I sometimes forget I'm lucky he's not hitting me. What did I do to deserve it? I must have done something that you don't do to men. But I can't remember what it was, and tiptoe into my future with my arm figuratively raised to ward off the blows. Things hit me is my paranoid belief. Falling nuts. Frisbees from way across a meadow. A beach ball. A bike on a dark path. A baseball bat. If I'm around and something's flying out of control, it comes my way. Including of course fists, and babies' hard heads. I got a split lip from one of the children's foreheads and everybody outside thought it was Hugo who did it.

Sometimes the two words—Christmas Day—had a chilling effect on her ears and eyes. Tinsel and pine awoke in her memory bank and rattled like coins. The little streets of old Quebec City tinkled in the same way—icicles from eaves, and down the steep cliff the rolling river, touched by brutish blocks of ice and timber, reminded her of the word RE-LENTLESS. They walked away from the plate glass window stocked with dildos, each with a hand on the double pram, silver and frosty. She felt the impression of pain like thumbs moving on her temples. He was wheezing asthmatically. A black three-quarter length coat and soggy but shiny black shoes. He had his leather satchel.

He began talking reactionary—We will send the children to the nuns when the time comes. . . . They need to be trained early to be chaste . . . . I like how tidy and clean it is up here, I like the feeling that the government is liberal but the country is conservative . . . . I came up here to try to make a new life, find a job. Why are you here? I knew you might come this way, given your tendency to head north whenever you run away from home, arrested adolescent that you are . . . bitch.

He batted her shoulder. She wore one of those long coats that stop just above the ankles, it was navy blue, and some of her hair—coarse black strands—shone against the fabric. She walked a little faster.

I want to stop this night-breaking misery we are in, he said.

You mean nightmarish?

Nightmarish. Don't you?

Well of course. Let's live separately.

We could share the same building but not the same rooms?

That's what I mean! You could have girlfriends, I wouldn't care.

But not get a divorce?

No, no divorce.

I don't really believe in divorce.

Now that we've had the babies, what's the point?

They "brightened" and "conversed" now on their way to the car. She doted on her babies and he was never mean to them, though he did not ever indicate a great deal of interest. At least he wasn't one of those cruel fathers, the ones you see everywhere, raging over their children in public places. He was indifferent to them, and only raged over her.

In the car heading south, they pretended they were able to control their destinies. They spoke about their lives with benign smiles. They built up a picture which made them both happy—of life in a duplex, him on one side, alone, with the children only when he wanted them; her on the other side, with the children most of the time and with her carpentry. With this huge balloon between them, they were kind to each other, considerate, and wished the best for themselves.

The children cooed happily in their car seats in back, three and four years old now, and the landscape whirred by like a winding sheet. Sad hope! Dream of a new marriage! If only it had worked, she would cry throughout the years. But the steady drip of grief, at these hopes' failure, never left her after that day.

That night they slept in a bed-and-breakfast attic room, with heaps of parti-colored quilts keeping out the chills, and the children between them. And the next morning, they went over the border back into Maine, and there she begged that he drive her to her little hometown by the sea, so she could take snapshots of some of the houses she had forgotten. He agreed benevolently, without jealousy, without impatience. He talked now about the social necessity of marriage, and contradicted all his theories of women and prostitution in the blimp of his joy. Their silver car whirred down the highway from the outside.

And in the inside, she was whirring with an inexplicable anxiety. Unlike him, she felt ruined. Stooped, plaintive, she lugged the girls over lumps of ice, and squatted with them beside her, while she snapped her pictures in the cold, quiet town. Like this she showed her true colors to the air—a mixed breed woman, squatting on the pavement, a native-born American alien in the Americas. One block of the town was being renovated by energetic hippies; their entrepreneurial tastes resulted in a wooden Indian restored on the steps of the general health food market. It was there that she offended him by something she said, and he got mad.

But this time it seemed to her, in her heart, that she was the one who had mapped their journey to this end. Not him. Because, as she cowered from his lifted hand, out of the store stepped a white man wearing a fur-collared suede winter jacket and big boots. When he saw her, he put down his bag and grinned. He said her name fondly. White smoke spun from his lips. His head nodded as if with approval as the father shoved her, and pulled a child away angrily. The white man pulled a knife from his inner hip and approached the husband. The husband then backed off, as if to receive a blow in private, out of sight of her, his face warped in a way she never saw before. She screamed and grappled for one daughter, the other one fell over on her side, beside the steps, and the white man slashed the coat of the husband. No blood was drawn. But she begged the white man to stop what he was doing; he ignored her. She ran into the store with the babies and squatted on the floor beside huge bags of cat food. People gathered at the window watching, and from them she learned what was happening. The husband was being hauled away by the cops, and the white man was explaining in what way he had been dangerous. She was shaking all over and crying too in dry heaves, the children were reaching for objects on shelves.

When the white man returned, he ushered her and them out of the store and into his car. It was obvious to everyone that she did not enjoy this rescue operation, but looked out the car window like a kidnapped child, seeking her father. What had happened wasn't fair. And she had led him there! Into a briar-patch of history's devising. No one really cared what her husband had done to her. He had been taken off by the police because he was a stranger and a shadow in that white town not because he had lifted his hand at her.

The white man brought her to the bus depot and bought her and the children one-way tickets home. As soon as they got there, she packed in a rush, full of errors, and ran away to another city. The father of her children put out a warrant for her arrest. She was wanted for kidnapping, then found. The idea was that he wanted to see and be with his children, and so she was put in place that was part prison for part crazy person, and the girls went to foster care to await a father who never came to claim them after all. In prison hospital she learned to make dollhouses, a trade she would pursue throughout the years. When she was freed, promising God that she would never marry again as long as she lived, she could not shake her fear that he would find her. Liberty and randomness were synonymous for her. She became a foot soldier and captain in her own solitary army, an army of three. With the children, now six and seven, on either side of her, she moved and moved again. And though she had to leave behind the dollhouses she made in prison, now she made much more elaborate ones, modelled on the houses in her childhood town. She sold them, reluctantly. They weren't really houses for dolls anyway, but spaces for her to live in.

She was Felicity Dumas, four feet eleven, with long black hair in braids, skin tone the pale brown of the inside of an owl's wing, nervous and birdish in gesture, with a thick ribcase and broad hips, with strong white teeth and strawberry pink lips. She always seemed to be elsewhere mentally, listening too acutely to a far-off sound, or remembering something someone said who wasn't even there. People couldn't get her to concentrate on them, it was maddening. If she saw a male configuration resembling her husband, she stopped, squinting, her shoulders stiff, and ran to hide wherever she could.

One day she really did see Hugo on the streets of Manhattan, near Soho, and he saw her. He was with another man, he looked happy, and she was disarmed for a few seconds, believing him trustworthy—father! But when he raised his hand to wave, she flinched, and hot-flashed. Now she saw him running after her, gun or hand raised, and like a woman having a seizure, she groped, stumbling, for the door of a cab, while her brain palpitated and hallucinated . . . . *She was walking down from the Walhalla Plateau to Cape Final in Arizona, where she could view the buttes, shrines and thrones of the Grand Canyon. What a basin of light and time! Colors and all weathers lived in that stilly and holy zone: from the most arid desert to the tip of Alpine peaks. Birds zoomed miles below her to their nests in the ruined pueblos dug into the walls. Reptiles, spiders, wildflowers coexisted there. But the density of silence was like a form of time she had never entered before, and it wouldn't let her stay there alive. So she jolted back into her senses, as if she had just been visiting the inside of her brain, its topology . . . .* The cab rattled and banged up the Bowery, and she looked in her address book for the name of that white man who had helped her before. It was a search and a gesture she repeated often. He was the same man who had often rescued her. But now it was not enough for her to see his name, because she kept her finger closed up in the little book for such a long time, it grew red and numb.

Before long she left Manhattan, taking the children out of school, and went back to the town in Maine where she last saw the white man. All she wanted was for him to rid her of the problem. Make me safe from the father of my children! He had made her safe from one thing and the other before. He rescued her by ruining her life in the way that some peo-

ple can do. His name was Temple, and since her teens he
served the function of boss, seducer, never-lover, and owner
of the world in which she was condemned to live.

Between guilt and fear, there is this tie, Temple told her. Do
you feel guilty for leaving him, or do you really fear him? Or
do you maybe fear what you want to do to him?

I really fear him, Felicity said. But I'm telling you this secret,
too. I made a promise to God that I would never marry
again, if the children and I could just be kept safe.

I've heard it's dangerous to make deals with God, he observed, and now she had a glimpse of his old charm: he listened for the pulse behind the words being spoken to him,
and measured it. Even if what he said was hurtful, at least it
was DEEP.

They were in the reconstructed bar he owned. He told her to
wait outside, where she could talk to a few old people from
her past. She did, but dreamily. Sometimes the world's substance seems a watery reflection of something more solid ex-
isting in the mind. Nothing is really out there. As she waited
for Temple to join her, she experienced this state of pictorial
distance. Voices were like echoes, without a location in flesh.
It was only a question of dreaming rather than being, though
she still could just manage the etiquette of life. Temple in the
past ascribed this quality to a genetic defect in her, a kind of
petit mal seizure. But now he told people it had to do with
environment. Certain places and people seemed to bring it
on. Himself being one of them. He looked at her now as if
she was a parchment made of honey and he was hungry.

Then he lurched towards her and assured her he would re-
move her husband from her life, without harming him. She
seemed not even to hear him, or care, but gazed at the glassy
branches dripping with sun. Rivulets of snow rushed down
the gutters. She listened to the sound as if gurgle was a language she could translate just by paying attention to it. He
said he would have her husband deported and the marriage
annulled, and now her face whitened to the same hue as his.
She wrote her guilt on the roof of her mouth with the tip of
her tongue: God forgive me! Meantime, her youngest child
was shivering and coughing while her sister tried to keep her
warm inside her coat and arms.

Two

Two years later she was sent to Boston—by the same white man—to stay with a friend of a friend of his. It was late winter. This friend—her host—was living with his dying father in order to take care of his mother. He was nearly young, a lawyer. He took Felicity in, with her two small children, because she was said to be homeless. And he was told that she would be a help with his sick father.

The apartment was a kind of infirmary—dingy and over-stuffed and smelling of paint thinner—for that time, and he was a kind of physician, a role he was not suited for, being nervous and private. She slept on a pullout couch with her children laid out on either side of her. She was tiny, black-haired, with sandcolored skin the rough texture of a drunk or drug addict. She carried pills and took them for her headaches—migraines, she said—and she managed each day to get the girls to the local elementary school—late—and pick them up late too.

She was very helpful in unexpected ways—cleaning up the kitchen and bathroom till they shone, then sitting at the window with a beer, just staring into the street. She helped his mother with his father—turning him over to change the soiled sheets, cleaning his pajamas, washing him in the most intimate ways. Her nostrils and lips tensed, but she otherwise showed no awkwardness or disgust in the face of disease.

One night, soon after her arrival, she told the lawyer that God would reward him some day for his hospitality to her.

29

He doubted that, and didn't say that she was herself repaying him with her actions.

Once she tried to describe to him the events which brought her to his door. He hardly heard her, he didn't want to hear her. All he could remember later was her description of a man who dominated her. She said, Watch out for him, he's dangerous. He doesn't look it either. Not like a pimp or a pirate or anything. He looks good—blond, blue-eyed, well-dressed, like a politician! The only special thing you could notice about him is he can't keep his head still. Some nerve damage, I guess. It nods a little. Like one of those dolls. Like this.

Watching her head nod heavily from side to side, like someone who listens to a sad story and responds with the negative sway of the head, he felt sorry for the dangerous man. Abruptly, he wanted to hear the whole account of her recent past over again, and she told him, repeating it all without a sigh or lapse in intensity. Again, he didn't really listen. She was, he realized, the smallest American woman he had ever seen. And her story—about love, food stamps, children, lost husband—was so big it was impossible to imagine her supporting it all.

His father died around twilight on a Saturday. That day snow covered Boston and its environs. The son spent the afternoon sitting by the sickbed reading aloud *Isaiah* and watching his father's exceptionally long fingers pluck at the blanket as if pulling off lint. The father was white, at least his complexion was pale if brown in patches, the skin papery. At five, in the blueing of the evening, when Boston's sky was lit with a gold sunset that illumined the snow, the son went out for a walk, and the father went into his final throes. The mother locked herself in the bathroom, covering her ears, like one who can't bear the screams of a birthing, and Felicity was left to help him cross over and out. She left her daughters watching television, and shut herself in the room with the old man, and held his head and shoulders over her knees, while he crackled and burned. She stared into his eyes and he into hers as he was dying, and when the immobility seized him, she felt a current pass into her own bones. She sat for a long time, as this sensation (like a low-level electric appliance humming in her hands) ran through her.

When the son came in, and found her like that, he stood at the end of the bed, wondering what her expression meant. She didn't say a word, though, but politely lay the father's shoulders and head down on the pillows, and left the room. Outside the city was hollowed by evening blue.

The next night the man left the house around six with Felicity and her two children. The two girls were obedient in the back seat. He took them to eat at a Mexican restaurant and then to a movie. Afterwards they all went to a motel to sleep. The man didn't want to be anywhere near his mother while she was in mourning. He had left her with old friends and had taken Felicity and her girls with him for no account-able reason beyond gratitude. Even as it happened he couldn't explain, either, why they all ended up in a motel. But there they were, and the girls slept on the floor on pil-lows borrowed off of chairs, while Tom and she shared the same medium-sized bed, and watched television. She con-sumed a four-pack of peach wine cooler, and smoked ciga-rettes. She told him that the last time she had had sex was when she conceived the youngest girl, who looked sickly. That was several years before.

How about you? she asked him.

About three years.

Wow. Do we qualify as virgins or not?

No. It takes seven years to be revirginated.

Who dropped that rule?

My brother Dan. He's a connoisseur in that regard. He went eight years without.

What is he, religious?

No, well, in a sense. Let's just say we had the same mother.

She seemed harmless to me.

You must be a poor judge of character.

Why didn't your brother help out?

Now? Well, he's my half-brother. My mother was married to another man, briefly. My father raised him, but Dan just stayed away as much as he could.

But even when your father was dying?

It's hard to explain.

The man looked at her in the light of the television. She gave off myriad emotions; he believed he would never understand a woman like her. The forceful chin, eyes heavily lidded, breasts round and firm on a boyish frame. And all that hair. And a baseball cap passed from child to child to her. He wouldn't dare touch her. Her unpredictability was frightening. He thought of her horrible life as he looked at her, then tried to assemble the parts for a life that was not horrible, and couldn't.

The night was memorable for its lack of completion. He lay awake watching television while she and the girls slept. This way he successfully avoided being present at his mother's first hours of grief, and at the same time avoided being present at his own.

Soon enough he was confronted with the difficulties of clearing out his father's possessions—clothes, shoes, papers. Each emptied article filled as he held it—with an immaculate presence, invisible and potent as a smell. The things that coated the skin, that served as protection from wind and sun, that kept the feet apart from the pavement—these were so pathetic as to make his eyes boil with tears of pity. A pair of bent and sloppy galoshes with rusty buckles made him twist with grief. Eyeglasses bent to fit the nose and skull. And then there were the papers.

He could not resist reading his father's notebooks, especially those dating back to the earliest years of his own childhood. And indeed here he discovered a piece of information which sent him into an ecstasy of curiosity. His father had written down the address of a federal prison where Dan's father was incarcerated. And he had done so more than twenty years before.

He was unable to speak to his mother about this news, because she was incapable of receiving negative information. Or so he had been taught. But he did mention it to Dan, on the phone, and Dan reacted by saying, "I don't want to know about it." So he was alone with a revelation which terrified him. If Dan's father was alive, in Southern California, and in prison, why was the story always told that he had disappeared "off the face of the earth?" The lawyer adored his own father, and thought of him as having an impeccable moral character—progressive, pacifist, honest. So next he called the federal penitentiary to discover if such a prisoner was there, still alive and well. Yes. Pedro was alive but very old in Southern California.

The lawyer began to fill up with dread now, and to wish he had not missed his father's dying hour, and to wish that he could ask him important questions. The silence of his absence horrified him. He couldn't accept the evaporation of a living body into empty space. He was scared he would forget his father's face. He began to wonder if Felicity Dumas, who had long since left with the friend who had brought her, could help him. He remembered her and the background comfort of her ministrations, and especially the moment she lifted a white wet cloth from his father's face and showed the impressions of two eyes, a nose and mouth intact there. He missed his father. He dreamed about Felicity holding the body at least three times, and she didn't seem as much a stranger as she should. He wanted to see her again—to fill in the empty space. And he called their mutual friend who said, "Strange. I was going to call you. To see if you wanted a paid vacation to San Diego. In exchange for a favor. It has to do with Felicity Dumas."

What about her?

"She needs help finding a place to live, and get settled. It seems she is incapable of dealing with life's daily demands, and requires guidance. Male guidance. She's not my problem, believe me, but a mutual friend—He'll pay your way."

The lawyer didn't ask why he had been selected for the job, but agreed to do it. The coincidental nature of the offer to see Felicity, and to go to San Diego, struck him with some suspicion, but it was the suspicion of superstition rather than paranoia. He couldn't believe how convenient the timing was. He thanked God.

I wanted to go there anyway, he told Jay (an English emigré, and dealer by trade and nature). Not because of her, but for a completely separate reason.

"Then good. Personally I'm surprised you'd agree to go at all," said Jay.

Believe me, it's a piece of luck.

"Let's hope your luck lasts. Anyway, she could use a bit of help. I'll let you know more soon."

There's nothing illegal involved, is there? asked the lawyer.

"You'd be the last person we'd send if there were. A lawyer?"

For several days, after work in a small legal aid office on the margins of Boston, the lawyer spilled his way through more notebooks by his father. Most of them were jottings about weather, current events, art shows, ideas for paintings, with wrinkled clippings stuck into the pages, unattached and falling. He could easily throw them all away. But then he found the partial transcript of a trial, officially copied onto legal size white paper which was now yellowing, and the transcript was a kind of official statement—by Pedro Dominique—Dan's father—almost a confession. It read:

"At age nineteen I was a member of the Marine Cooks and Stewards Association—a Communist-controlled union. Afterwards I enlisted in the US Army where I found out all I needed to know about race and class. When I was stationed in Texas I was given some Marxist literature to read. Most of it concerned class issues in Britain. I hate the English. In New York, during the Soviet-Nazi Nonaggression Pact, I went to rallies where the speakers were German Bundists and American Communists. I agreed with their conclusions. It was in San Francisco I got my Communist literature from the Party bookstore—the Maritime Bookshop. Later I was discharged from the Army and got seamen's papers in San Diego. This was where I got involved with the National Maritime Union and became a card-carrying member of the Party. Do what you want about that. In 1944 I signed on the troop ship USS *Brazil* in Boston. Conditions on board those ships was sickening, with ten men sleeping in one badly ventilated fo'castle. One cold storage egg apiece every Sunday, it stank, the only fruit an orange once a week, moldy meat, mush full of weevils, no linen—for $25 a month. I never forget the odor from dirty sweaty clothes, or the stench of leaking oil. On that ship I was surrounded by militant pro-Communists for several months. I won't tell you who they were, so don't bother asking. They were great men. Then in Boston I met a woman and got her pregnant with my son Dan. Together we became acquainted with a printer who introduced me to some more fellow travellers, and I considered this man my first true friend. Under pressure from the government I changed unions and got a membership in the Marine Firemen, Boilers, Wipers and Watertenders Association and shipped out of Boston as an electrician. It was just about 1948 when the House Un-American Activities Committee began to hound me, as you obviously know already, and I was threatened with loss of citizenship and deportation. I went back to Boston to seek legal help, but my best friend by then was shacked up with my woman and my son and he wanted me out of town. I guess just about everybody did by then. So I went West. I changed my identity. And to this day I still believe—"

The transcript ended there.

Three

In a matter of weeks the lawyer found the woman sitting on a curb with her two girls, in southeast San Diego. He drove by her once, did a U-turn, staring, drove by again, did another U-turn, and returned slowly, pulling up alongside her knees. He pretended to be amazed by this encounter.

She stood up and walked around to his window, squinting, and then her face shifted in relief and surprise.

I don't believe it, she said. Fuck 'n shit.

Neither do I.

What the hell are you doing in these parts?

Vacationing.

You?

Me too, he said. How are the girls? They look the same but bigger.

Already? You came in the nick of time. Can we hitch a ride?

Sure, get in.

The girls climbed, brown and smiling, into the back seat of the rental car. They remembered him with shy hellos. She was brown too now and her skin was smooth, clear. The only mark in her face was the kind of lining that comes with a lot of sun. As she gave him directions to her home, she examined him until he was ashamed and reddened.

So? What are you looking at? he asked.

You're paler than me.

I guess I am.

I used to be paler than you, she said.

She pressed her forearm against his to prove her point. The man, whose name was Tom, was dressed in shorts, a tee-shirt and sneakers. His skin was Mediterranean brown, and rough, as if he had fished daily on the high Atlantic for many years. But his mouth was soft, red, even delicate, and his expression distant and alarmed. He had a perpetual shadow of a beard, no matter how often he shaved. He was slender, his posture set back, tense and uncomfortable, as if he had been a fat child who never believed he was really thin. His arms and chest were hairy, but his hands were long, gentle and nervous. Felicity looked at him frequently, whenever they were together, as if to see which part of his person was in the foreground for that time.

They drove to the shack she inhabited. It was a small stucco building stuck behind suburban houses, and gardens gleaming with palm trees and bougainvillea. There was one bedroom and a tiny kitchen and bathroom. The girls slept on a pullout couch. But the place seemed barely occupied by anyone. A box of books lay unpacked on the floor; there was a small black-and-white t.v. and a few plastic dishes. The girls' toys were mostly of a boyish robot variety—bright-colored steel figures you could assemble in multiple forms. They lay scattered on the pullout bed. Tom stood at the door and asked her a question he had had in his mind since his father died.

Did my father say anything before he died?

Something about ferns, she said. Want a beer?

No thanks. What about ferns?

Something about keys and ferns being the same.

They look alike?

No, I don't think so. More like "the key to life is a fern." I don't remember exactly. That doesn't sound right. Sorry.

No. That's good enough. Thanks.

I still think it's strange, you showing up like this. You're sure nobody sent you to spy on me?

Why would they?

They just might. That man might. The one I guess I told you about.

With the shaking head?

Yeah, exactly.

I don't know him, so you can relax.

It's just so lucky, you know. I mean, today they're evicting us. I was out looking for a temporary shelter when you came along. If only you knew how hard it is to find a place if you're a single mother. Everyone hates us. We drive people nuts, just looking at us. They think my kids will rip the wallpaper off the walls, or something, just because there isn't a man in the house.

Where do you want to go now?

You tell me.

Money isn't your only problem. What else is going on? What does the shaking head man want?

I can't tell you. You must be judging if you're a lawyer.

I'm not.

You always look really tense and abashed at the same time. I can't imagine you up in front of a justice.

You don't have to. I never will be.

So what do you want to do with us?

You can come along to my motel, and we'll figure it out. I owe you one.

You gave us a place to stay already.

Big deal. You washed my father when he was dying.

She shrugged with her palms upraised and an expression of astonishment on her face.

Again they ended up in a motel, this time the one he was vacationing in, near Sea World. Outside a freeway was in constant use on one side; on the other was a view of Mission Bay, stiff jelly blue. Palm trees sprouted tall and thin as asparagus, or else sat squat as pineapples along the sand. Boats ripped up the water. The girls played in the wet sand and walked in the water until late at night and then they slept, again on the floor, while Tom and Felicity again watched television, side by side in a bed.

They talked. He told her his father had been haunting him.

Wow, so tell me, she said.

You won't laugh?

Go on.

Okay. Three times he's appeared in powerful dreams. Once emerging from a crowd outside. It was like a wedding party in the twilight of a strange hotel. Carrying his big hat. Then I saw gray shadows on a tree trunk in a town called John or Jude and they turned into him. Once, by Hell, where the air was like a dirty barge, he carried luggage. Each time he looked exhausted but astonished. He had been, he always said, away on a trip and never expected to stay away so long. He really just wanted to apologize and let us get on with our lives.

Were you scared?

I kept staring at the space he had physically occupied long after he was gone. Always I wondered what it felt like to be him dying. Was he terrified? Relieved? Obedient?

Why are you here anyway? Tell the truth.

To look for my brother's father. He's in prison out here—east of here. I have to see him. My brother won't.

Here, give me some room, was her response.

Move your legs then.

There. Now?

The pillow. I'm the one who cares about it.

So take it. I'll sleep on my arm.

I'm not going to lay a hand on you.

Now the ashtray? Why not? she asked and flirted withher hair.

I don't know you. You may be full of disease. Did you smoke when you were pregnant?

Not as much. Tell me about your brother Dan.

Did you drink?

Just a couple of beers a day. Or Champale.

You're lucky you didn't mess up your children. I mean, they seem fine though Matty still looks kind of weak. Is there anything seriously wrong with them? with her?

As far as I'm concerned, they're perfect.

Who was the father?

I thought I told you all that. Before, she said.

To be honest, I forget, forgot. I never thought I'd see you again after that weird night in the motel.

And here we are again. I remember you always talked about your brother.

That's right. My brother Dan. I did?

So who's your girlfriend now?

When you ask me that it makes me think you want to come on to me, and I really don't want you to, so let's not talk about things like romance.

Fine, I'm going to sleep anyway.

She buried herself under the covers beside him, carefully avoiding contact under the sheet.

I hate the smell of motels, she said, but at least I'm safe, thank you.

I thought you were going to smoke.

No, I'm going to sleep instead, she said.

Tom lay awake for two hours in a state heightened by wild thoughts of home and future. Something in Felicity's spirited candor made his voice rise from his chest, and an urge to articulation follow. He was usually quiet. But he had an invisible tongue in which he talked to himself. When he tried to voice his thoughts to others, he felt as if a long chute—a kind of upside-down cornucopia—led from his brain to his mouth. The words fell too fast, or got stuck. It was the descent from his mind to the vernacular which caused him greatest trouble.

In the morning she was sitting by the window, with a lighted match held up in the air, one after the other. She would light one and blow it out. She was crying inside the veils of her thick black hair. He watched her, again surprised by how small she was. With her legs exposed, he could guess she was about four feet eleven. He couldn't see her face.

Are you trying to set the room on fire?

I'm praying, she said.

For what? And what have the matches got to do with prayer?

I don't have any candles.

What do you want me to do with you today?

I guess take us to a shelter. First tell me about your brother. Tell me a story.

I don't have one ready.

Shit. Typical. You can't just invent one. How come you're a lawyer?

I'm interested in politics, in this country, you know, and the question of human freedom. Civil rights, civil liberties. I just wake up and smile when I think in those terms. Politics is my single passion. I inherited it from my parents, but have a very different view from theirs. I don't care much about anything else.

What did your parents believe in? I remember they were kind of poor which means they were probably Democrats which means you must be conservative which wouldn't surprise me.

Believe me, you're way off the mark.

> Well, go on and tell me how your parents were, she prod-
> ded, lighting up a shoelace, and spitting on it.

Tom put his hand to his throat as if to dislodge his own
breath; it was a gesture swift and accurate.

Actually it was my brother Dan who opened my eyes to
them. One night, in the winter, he and I were walking on the
other side of the street from them in Boston. They were with
their usual pack of friends, and Dan said they looked like
Fellini characters, that they were all second-rate in what they
did, or worse, they were losers. Look at them, look at them,
he kept saying, and I never could look at them the same way
again.

> That makes him sound kind of like a shit.

No. Just realistic.

> But is Dan such a winner?

That's not the point. He's uncluttered. They were cluttered,
collectors of kitsch, they dragged their pasts around with
them like bags of old newspapers. And they believed that
they were brilliant and misunderstood. Only in Boston can
you get such a combination of snobbery and ruin.

Sometimes you sound like a snob yourself. Your father was really nice to me. Even when he was feeling so sick, he was polite. That counts for a lot. Tell me about him, and your mother. Go on. I like to listen.

Are you sure?

What else have I got to do? It comforts me.

Well, you could see that we had no money. My father was a printer whose office was down near Chinatown and South Station. He printed flyers, pamphlets, one advertisement newsletter and a four-page leftist newspaper. At night and on weekends he painted in oils—dark images of urban life (red brick brownstones, stooped humans, the El, cars, that kind of thing) or delicate ferns, pastel-colored. He was fifteen years older than my mother. And Pedro. His life seemed to have no beginning, though he came from the South. There was a quality of timelessness to him because of his age. He was a kind and quiet man, as you could tell, whose favorite subject was liberty and how to pursue it.

So how did he meet your mother?

He served in the US Army during World War Two, was stationed in North Africa for most of that time, and spoke often of playing baseball outside of Tripoli with an all-black unit. Apparently the three years in combat changed him from a New Dealer into something more internationalist, or radical. In any case, he met my mother in Boston, later, when she was working with the C.P. She was at the first meeting he attended, but she was with Pedro already, they were lovers, they never really married, and he felt sorry for them both and took them home to feed them. I don't think he and my mother fell in love until long after they were friends. He had just inherited his print shop from his father, and it became the center of political dialogue among anarchists, Trotskyites, Democrats and others. Deep down in Post Office Square he printed leaflets and pamphlets and a theater newspaper. He had many white friends at work, but he was always obsessed with race issues. Pedro was his best friend, Pedro, by the way, being black, and many years his junior. This fact and his political alliances kept lots of customers away, and he had a limited number of friends. But my father accepted this isolation with the same irony and good humor that drew other people to his shop. My mother was not so good-humored, and it was, after all, a really thick male environment. She must have felt excluded. My father was never up to her cynical wit. She had an Irish tongue, a kind of competitive conversation ruled her social contacts. Who could be the funniest and the meanest the fastest.

But wait a minute. How did she switch from Pedro to your father? What happened?

My parents really didn't talk about that. It was kind of a forbidden topic. Anything about Pedro was treated as unfit for human conversation. When I was born, and for a few years after, Pedro was still in the picture, but off to the side, and I don't really get the chronology or its meaning. But he would take Dan and me out with him. He was like an uncle—a poor one—who was humored, but rejected. My mother had been mentally ill as a teenager, and something in her nature made everyone bow and kowtow to her, as if we all feared she would go totally berserk if she was criticized, or if she received harsh facts. She ruled the house with this unarticulated dread. All I know is, my father became a pacifist, and my mother made him withdraw from political action, after Pedro disappeared, or just before, I'm not sure. She had a horror of the Friends of Progress, Mankind United, the Ku Klux Klan, the Umberto Nobile Fascio, the German-American Bund, and the group headed by Gerald K. Smith. She thought these groups were dangerous to her personally! She thought they would come and kidnap Dan. She even suggested that Pedro was a counter-subversive. She said, when he disappeared, that he was probably being sent abroad to work for the CIA. I tell you, she was not harmless, and Dan moved away from home at age sixteen, just to get away from her. Our whole house, all through my early childhood, was sick with talk about the meaning of "un-American." My mother scrutinized every organization to classify it according to whether it was created and controlled by Communists, or infiltrated and controlled? Was it Communist dominated, and infiltrated but not controlled? Or was it Communist infiltrated only for purposes of espionage? . . . And behind it all was the question of Pedro. Was he a spy, and a traitor, and would he return to destroy them?

I guess she felt guilty, said Felicity simply. I mean, after all, she dumped Pedro for his best friend.

At night as a child I lay awake, plagued with these images which were like seeds, thrown forward into a field of air. I saw my mother's fears bearing hideous future fruits.

That's why you have that look in your eye.

The girls began to stir, and soon they took over. Straight black hair, high cheekbones and wide pink lips, they could have been Arab, Latin, Pakistani. They rolled all over their mother who kissed them passionately and listened attentively to whatever each one had to say, no matter how trivial. If one of them whined, however, she got screamed at or smacked on the bottom as she flew by. A man who loved her would have to make room for these girls too, and learn to spend a lot of time outside that trio, without jealousy. He told her that. They watched television while Tom went downstairs and got them donuts and juice. On his return he walked around them with an expression of pleasure that he seemed unaware of feeling.

Why do shoelaces taste salty? Felicity asked him.

Lots of things do, he replied.

> We could make a banquet of all the things we tasted when we were kids. Towels . . . kneecaps . . . soles of shoes. . . . What else?

Jump ropes. The skin of a football—and a baseball. They were salty, like shoelaces.

> Pencils are salty.

So are some erasers.

But paper has the blandest taste of all. Like rice.

It would be good to make such a banquet, Tom said.

Felicity stared at his face, while he looked off into space somewhat self-consciously.

How many times did your mother get married? she asked.

Twice. Sort of. I mean, she never really married Pedro.

Which of the men did she love the most?

My father.

Which son did she love the most?

My brother.

I thought so. Where did you live all your life? In that same place I met you?

No. We lived in an even drearier place, way downtown.

And Pedro?

Pedro? He lived in a pit down in the South End. Near the project where my mother grew up. Near Holy Cross Cathedral. Do you know any of these places?

Sort of. I spent a little time in Boston, here and there.

Something like that. What about your people?

Anarchists.

That might be an accurate word for my parents too.

She and the girls disappeared into the bathroom and the shower, and Tom stood at the window watching herds of cars thunder down the freeway. He rubbed the bristles on his cheeks and his eyes took on an opaque look, inward-turning. The hoods of cars evoked obsolescence even as they raced before his eyes in different shapes. What's modern about the past? Some things are finished at the moment of completion. Technology. And even some relationships—they are done at the moment of consummation. . . . His mind was a swarm of word-sized figures and his face lapsed into an expression of deep familiarity with what passed behind his eyes, and how to get there.

What Tom could not tell Felicity:

TOO FAR would be his name for those long winters and the words in them, which stretched the margins of thinkable thoughts. Snow stuck to the bricks, whitening all that was red, and lined up on wires and ivy tendrils. Yellow daffodils and tulips drooped with their mouths ajar on their kitchen table. Books and oil paints smelled up the house. Dan sharing a room with him. The parents in the only other bedroom. Pedro, in the earliest years, walked through the drifts under the tracks to visit. After he disappeared, the mother made Dan share the bedroom with her and the father, fearing that Dan would be stolen in the night.

When Dan left for New York, Tom was bereft. Each winter after, near Christmas, he would come home and they would all go to a Greek restaurant downtown for dinner. Dan wore a black overcoat, with the collar turned up and hunched over, like the mother, and looked cold, like her, in the speeding snow. Tom held onto the cloth on his sleeve and stayed close to him. His skin and black curls, long-fingered hands and slender wrists, his cologne and his subtle sidewinding smile, his garnet brown eyes under heavy lids and a tentative way of speaking—all these made him seem heroic and foreign to Tom.

I remember the streets were always glitzy for Christmas. The more vulgar the better, Dan liked to say, and together he and I exclaimed over the silver and gold tinsel drippings and the artificial trees in the department store windows.

But you should see New York, he kept telling me. This is all like an imitation of the real thing. You should get Mum to bring you to see FAO Schwartz, Rockefeller Plaza and all the windows down Fifth Avenue, if you really want to see Christmas. Boston is like a toy city after New York. It's a poor man's imitation of a city. When you're in New York, you don't have to dream of being anywhere else in the world. Not Rome, not Paris even.

I dropped his sleeve and slowed away from his pace, walking alone between the lot of them. Always I knew that Dan was the real one and I was the fake, that he was the original and I was the print, that he was the winner and I had lost, that he was Manhattan and I was Boston, that he was wine and I was water, that he was coffee and I was tea, that he was art and I was business, that he was the soul of my mother and I was the body. But my eyes stung with salt in the white cold flakes because he had all but come out and said so.

He was sensitive and slowed to walk with me again, saying that he had a vision of my future. He said he could see me living in a one-room basement studio up near Harlem when I grew up. I would go to jazz concerts and otherwise live like a monk, or a hermit. I would be an artist of some kind, but he couldn't say which. Every day will be like a package that you will wrap up and deliver to the world, he said. You'll be the one everyone waits for at parties. And when you leave, which will always be early after arriving late, the party will disintegrate. You will be political and will be a leader of the poor . . . .

In my childhood hard winters moved into town with great, driving storms and fields of white to cross on foot. There was a beauty to those days: warmth indoors with the harsh snow ticking on the windowpanes, glass vases with the flowers brought home from Haymarket, music on the record player, tea. My parents had good mad friends who stayed around, other women who had children, men who were misfits and artists, and sometimes there was actually a pervading joy in the house. The radio played constantly, news coming in brought shouts and dialogue.

And spring in the little park up the street—rose-colored crab apple, weeping cherry, flowering judas which is purple, blushing apple blossoms, white dogwood, early lilac, red and yellow tulips, bunches of violets and a meadow of soft dandelions Around these, a black fence, cement, voices—

And now all I can pore over, inside the morning papers, is a statistic: one out of every twenty-one black males is murdered in this country. Many of the remaining ones are in jail. And all I can feel, in a visceral way, is the sickness of facts. I don't understand how it came to this.

Where is justice, I keep asking. It doesn't do any good to lock anyone up. Longer and longer sentences are handed out, millions of dollars are spent to prosecute offenders who will be out on the streets again soon. Young dealers, boys and girls, are given terribly long sentences for their crimes—longer sentences than any of the rich will ever get. And what is it like in a detention home? Six feet by ten feet, furnished with a single bed, a desk bolted to the wall, a stool, a toilet, a barred window, outside an enclosed yard containing twenty identically dressed kids. If a kid is lucky he'll be in the care of the Youth Authority where they can eat chips, candy, and Cup o' Soup and buy cigarettes and smoke them. In Juvenile Hall you aren't even allowed a pencil. In both places they are so crowded they have to join a gang for self-preservation. I want to be happy but I can't with this information—the experience of it—in my bloodstream. . . .

Now Felicity and the girls emerged from the bathroom with rosy and moist faces. Felicity came and stood by Tom to look out the window. He pointed out a cloud in the sky which resembled a fishbone and asked her what it looked like to her.

Snow, she said. I miss snow. Why do you look so mad?

My mind. It's racing.

Raging?

He shrugged.

Actually you look sort of like a saint—Peregrine maybe, or, no, Saint Sebastian. Crazy mad. Way out there.

Please, he protested.

What I mean is I think I can trust you.

Really? I wonder why.

There's some stuff I want to talk about.

Don't you have a lover?

Nobody will ever love me again.

You don't seem to need it anyway.

You're not the first person to say that. Can I braid your hair?

Okay but don't be seductive. I can't stand seduction.

See, you are a candidate for canonization. I bet you cut your tangles out with scissors. I bet you hardly ever use a comb.

He sat on the edge of the unmade bed and she crouched, knees up, behind him. She was dressed in her jeans again and a checkered shirt, and her hands were rough and competent at the same time. He felt her breath on the back of his ear like a hair. She asked if she could hack off the end of his hair with a knife.

It's a little rough along the edges, she explained.

Come on, just braid it and be done with it. Am I really taking you to a shelter? Is this something you do often?

No. I've only had to do it a couple of times.

Why do you live down here?

I heard there was good medical care.

For who?

No one. I just like to be near good doctors. I'm neurotic.

The best hospitals are in New England. You could have stayed there.

When I was first pregnant, she said, I stayed around New England. But then I had to run away from the father who was acting crazy. So I went to live on this island. Indian summer. I lived like a dog. When a woman turns into a dog, you can be sure she's near to God. My primary relationship then was with God. I still wish it was.

Where in New England? What island?

Up in Maine. But it got too cold, and he found me. The good thing about here is you can sleep outdoors if you get desperate.

That's a strange way to choose where you live. Especially when you have kids.

I lack the will to make money.

What do you have the will for?

I make dollhouses, but they've all been sold.

Do you believe society owes you a living?

I don't think in big terms like that. I'm on my own.

So what are you going to do?

It makes me cry to think about it. I don't know.

She gave a final efficient tug to his braid and let it fall with a thud at the nape of his neck. The girls stared into the television but moved their bodies restlessly. Tom said, Let's go.

In the rented car he began to take note of the littlest girl, who was one of those children who say wild and unexpected things. Her skin color was poor, as if she had rubbed buttercup juice into her cheeks, but her eyes were feverishly bright. Black as olives, and awestruck in their expression. She wiggled constantly, and whenever they walked, she hopped, skipped, jumped, then sank to the ground in a heap of thin bones, tired. Her hair started out neat and ended up messy in a matter of minutes. She chattered. If he listened, he could hear lines of surrealistic poetry coming from her, though she seemed to have no expectations of anyone listening to her at all. She didn't like to be touched much, but darted away from outstretched hands. This made her all the more tempting, and both her sister and mother were constantly reaching for a kiss, which she evaded.

The two girls sat in the back seat engaged in an intense battle using small plastic men. They had the air conditioning on, the windows rolled up. Outside: Plaza Boulevard—a dull yellow brick strip of commerce—and hot sun. The flat sandy terrain seemed to reject weight. The houses and shops were tacky, temporary shelters compared to the fortressed architecture of other cities. Taco and tortilla stands abounded; it was all but Mexico. Felicity wanted to cross over the border but he wouldn't go. She sulked and called him a drag, insisted on stopping to get some burritos and then slumped into talk about public education with her knees up on the dashboard. He was not listening, but cast critical glances at the beer can she held inside a styrofoam cup. They passed two shelters for the homeless and soup lines gathered outside dun-colored churches.

In the fall the children will go to school, don't worry, she told him.

I'm only worried about now, not then. You'll end up in a rehab center for alcoholics and your children in foster care if you don't watch your drinking.

I know, you're right.

So let's drive up to the mountains.

Yeah, let's go to Julian, she called over her shoulder.

The girls rejoiced at this mention of a town called Julian and she rearranged her posture to give directions. Driving, he rubbed the center of his forehead with the tips of his fingers as if he had a headache. He asked her to tell him the story of her life; his expression was cautious as he waited and she talked.

I'm an Army brat, she said without hesitation. I lived everywhere. My Dad was a spy. We went to Trieste, Germany, the Guadalcanal, the Far East, Texas, Seattle, Oklahoma, Fort Dix, Florida, San Diego, D.C., back to Texas and back to Panama. I went to nineteen different schools, travelled all over Europe and the Middle East. We even went to Egypt and to Japan, Hawaii, Micronesia! But I always spent my summers in Maine, in our house by the sea there.

Lies, said Tom. All lies.

How did you know?

You told me a completely different story before, he said.

All right, all right, that was the life story of the mean man, Temple, the one who's always after me.

Why tell his story? Get yourselves confused?

No, let's just say I was testing you. To see if you remembered anything I said before. You know about my childhood. Lee, tell him our life story!

Lee leaned forward, her face serious, even sad. She was the worrier in the group, the one who checked the time, and made sure none of them was being offensive to the outside world. She was as tender as a mother towards her mother and her sister, and showed little regard for herself. Her voice was measured, soft, insistent on getting facts correct:

Our father lives far away. Where he was born. He's a mixture of Indian and Portuguese. He's very smart, probably a professor. Definitely a poet. But he was in the rug business when he was with us. Mama had to stay in a hospital for awhile—

That's why I like the medical world so much, Felicity quickly interjected.

—and Matty and I lived with a foster family. Then she went to college and almost got a degree in hotel management. But we didn't have enough money so she stopped. We've travelled a lot—

Tons and tons! Matty called from behind. My father lives on the seashells. Pink ones and toenails.

To Boston, New York, Canada, New Hampshire, Connecticut, Arizona, Mexico, California, and where else?

Maine, said Matty. Where Mama was born.

Maine. She likes borders, said Lee. So she likes being near the border of Canada and near the border of Mexico.

She likes seashells too. She sells seashells by the seashore. She might meet our father on the beach someday.

No, Matty, she will not, said Lee.

Okay, that's enough, Felicity told her. Let's not get morbid.

The girls leaned back together and continued to play their war games with sounds hushed so they could tune in on the conversation in the front seat too.

Well, I guess that gives me some idea, said Tom. But I remember before, you told me about the nodding head man, and how he used to break up all your relationships.

Yeah, but let's not talk about that now, she whispered, indicating the children in the rear.

You and I have one friend in common.

Jay. He's no friend of mine, said Felicity. He's just what they call a contact. From what I hear he's one of these English types who comes over here and takes advantage of stupid Americans with his accent.

That's right. They ask him to do commercials on the radio, so the product will have the royal stamp on it. And really he's sleaze.

No. We don't have any friends in common. That's what makes it really strange that you're here, she remarked.

Well, I have my reasons. It's not really strange. I want to meet Pedro. In prison. And I have political interest.

But why stick with me?

It's better than being alone.

What's the political interest?

The same as everyone's. Law and order.

I hate the law, she said.

And I hate the order. I mean, the way things stand.

But why isn't your brother looking for his father? Why you? Self-interest is generally at the heart of most matters, she added.

I'll tell you why, said Tom, and nervously touched his throat. The two girls leaned up on the back of the seats then, their faces hanging over like donkeys in a barn. Matty put her hand around Tom's braid, and played with it while he talked. Outside they passed round brown hills, then rose up into the small mountains, greener from trees.

"Just before he disappeared, Pedro came to my school one day and took me for a long walk. We went to the Public Garden and watched the swanboats from the little bridge there. Everywhere I stepped his shadow covered me. His eyes were bloodshot, he had obviously been weeping, his whole face had that collapsed look, and he said that everyone would forget him—even his own son—when he was gone, and if he died, he would be forgotten, but even faster—and he said to me that I, of all of them, must never forget him, never let him 'rot in hell'—those were his words."

Why you?

He said that I at least had a chance at getting power in this world. Something to that effect. And I should be sure to take responsibility for him when I got that power. What a laugh.

When did you find out where he was? asked Felicity.

Only recently, and by chance. When I was going through my father's papers. That's the horrible part. My father knew where Pedro was all that time.

What's so horrible?

Pedro was his best friend. He should've kept in touch at least.

What for? Your father had run off with his wife and son. Why would he want to keep in touch with him? Self-interest rules, I tell you. It always does.

God, Felicity. You sound so cynical. Not like yourself.

But she was right, about self-interest, his, the way women are. They make these extravagant statements; you have to argue with them, you have to put them down; then, later, you realize they were right. At that point it's a matter of honor, whether you're going to steal their ideas or go back to them, apologize and congratulate them for being so smart. I didn't say anything to her, but my self-interest was obvious enough to me. I wanted to know the worst about my parents so I could finally be free of their influence.

We ate our way through Julian, preserved as a ghost town for tourists. Apples were the staple of the town's industry. The signs for pies were everywhere. With wooden porches and homey storefronts, the idea was to keep Julian as alive as a Hollywood stage set for a Western. The girls were happy. I left them all eating ice cream and pie and went for a walk down the side roads and into a grove of silvery blue eucalyptus trees. The sky was vague. I sat on a rock to smoke and think. It was soft and quiet there, the shadows a pale dapple of green, like those of houseplants on a white wall. I was glad to be among trees again. Southern California seemed barren to me, except for the comedy of palm trees. I missed the sudden heaps of green and shadow, armloads of dots dancing in the air. But now I felt another atmosphere—a thicker one— behind me, and stood and turned. My father's ghost in broad daylight.

You came all this way for me? I marvelled.

He looked, as he had before, exhausted, and carried the gray bag. His posture was straight but his features were dusty and limp. He explained, again, that he had only been away on a trip, had never expected to stay so long. He was not mad that we had gone on with our lives in the meantime. He only wanted to apologize for the length of his stay and to make a few remarks.

Ferns repeat each other superficially, like keys. In reality, every fern is unique. The ground is a door, the ferns are locks. But why are we put here if only to die? Why not begin and end with space and leave earth out of the picture altogether?

He gazed at me vacantly, and I tried to speak to him before he could become a cloud or a shade, but he was gone before I stopped stammering. He left me hobbled with grief. Everything was the color of tears and rain—drained of variation. No green. Again and again I could not recover from that loss, but in each effort to replace his absence with an interest or object, he intervened reminding me of my duty to him. I didn't know who I was without my father.

Nothing about a fern resembles a lock, but a key can be imaged in the purfled edges, even though soft and green, not hard and gold. Even the fossil of a fern in a cowpad would not resemble the shape of a lock. Yet the fern reminds me of something relevant to a way in. It barely exists but seems, instead, to be inscribed: the replica of an original, something denser, darker, damper. Its liquid postures and invention of a tip, after an organized retreat in a cone's shape, makes it a metaphor for the spine and spirit endlessly aspiring. It is organized, more so than most forest greens which have a tendency to twist and crawl en masse around themselves, bark and stone. The fern is orderly and shy like a lock intended only for the one who holds the key. My father collected, pressed and painted ferns. I always wondered why.

They were ripping at red licorice ropes on the steps of a bakery when Tom returned. The sun was cooling and the shadows were darker. She squinted up at him and asked him what took so long. His eyes looked puffy. Had he fallen asleep? she asked. He said yes and asked what they would like to do next.

The water, the kids want to see some water.

Okay, guys, let's go, he agreed, steering them to the car. The littlest girl held onto his belt crossing the street. He held the hand of Lee, the older one, while Felicity scrambled around in her enormous bag for another can of beer.

They drove south and west to the coast. The Coronado Bridge was the turquoise of a swimming pool. From there they could see all the way to National City, to Mexico. The Hotel Del Mar was too expensive for them and they circled through the parking lot watching the tourists fumble with enormous cars. Then they got lost by Border Field State Park where helicopters were circling the sloughs, and egrets barked like small terriers.

Over some boulders the ocean lashed, panted, exhaled, inhaled all the way down to the border. They walked there by the Tijuana Slough Refuge and the sea. Surfers danced on the waves or lay like dolphins—black shiny dots in a splendor of passivity. The sand curled up like an unpressed hem, and the fencing, intended to keep out Mexicans, stopped before the beach began. Anyone could walk in and out of Mexico along the shore. The backyards of Tijuana were exposed, and above the beach was an American park filled with Mexicans eating lunch and listening to music. Farther along, the shoulder of Tijuana, scruffy as an old dog, tumbled into America, to stables for thoroughbred horses, black and brown and elegant horses, and into flat green farms of Instant Grass.

The air is very sweet here, said Tom.

It's Mexican air all the way from here to Oceanside. It's un-American air.

Tell me what's really happening, Felicity.

Now?

Why not? I want to understand.

It's so hard to trust you. I mean, if I hadn't loved my father, I wouldn't trust any men. Too bad I loved him then. It led to nothing but pain.

Don't be so bitter. It doesn't suit you.

If you knew.

Then tell me.

It has to do with Matty.

What about her?

Felicity leaned over and whispered, *She's dying,* into his ear. He felt a line of cold follow the words down his spine. She said she would tell him later, when they were alone, the story.

Four

That night Felicity told Tom that she had been travelling, for many months, from one city to another, looking for a hospital to care for her daughter. Matty needed a new liver to extend her life for a few years, during which time a cure might be found for her condition. Felicity had had no success in finding a transplant; they were hard to come by; and the poverty of the family did not make them prime candidates for a donor. She gave up hope about a year before.

Then Temple, who always had a sixth sense about her, found her in Boston, and called her down to where he was staying. He had heard about her daughter's illness; he thought he could help her.

Always he had known the exact moment when Felicity was about to go broke, and he wired her money; or he knew when she was about to be happy with someone else, and he stepped in and destroyed the relationship with lies, innuendoes, threats. Sometimes—as on her escape to Quebec—she called him out to rescue her. In earlier centuries whales and wolves and plague played the role that Temple played in her life; so did the gods. She had learned how to appease and how to avoid and how to exploit him. But after he had her husband deported, something changed, and she no longer knew which tricks to play to get her way. There was nobody left inside his body who made sense to her, in terms of a personal history. He still did everything on time, and kept his promises, but these seemed like deformities against the solid and cruel front he projected.

With some dread she left the children in Boston and went to meet him in New York. They met outside a movie theater and the same illumination that was always circling his head was there, but now she felt the aura contained a substance as lethal as radiation. She kept a small distance between them, and they went inside the theater.

The lights to her seemed to dim and brighten again several times. Temple leaned against her. She drew a deep breath and decided to respond to him as she always had, in order to get from him what she wanted. He liked to talk about money. She tried to make him laugh by wisecracking about that subject he held so dear.

A five dollar bill is my favorite, she said. I don't know why. And so is a nickel. There aren't too many of either of them. But that's not it. Five is friendly.

In Australia they're making plastic money now. Can you imagine what that will do to our idea of money?

Play money. I once had food stamps.

Twice, he said.

Twice, and they were like that. Monopoly.

What's the value of an hour of your time?

Something in plastic.

It's all imaginary, anyway, said Temple. Always was. Now shh.

The lights thinned, the screen went white and music came out from the walls. Her anxiety was making her sick. She tried to control it. To be in the dark, with Temple in a movie theater—nearly empty because of the hour—was making her cheeks stiff around her teeth. It was a distorted smile. She squeezed her cheeks so her lips bowed and looked to the right so he wouldn't see. You wouldn't begin to understand such a gesture if you've never made it yourself. There are landscapes in America, separated by hundreds of miles, which are all but identical. There are Main Streets you couldn't tell apart. Grain elevators, drive-ins, wooden houses with a dignity and simplicity which affirms function above decoration and a kind of humbling under the clouds. And a citizenry becoming more nomadic with each passing hour.

But they were on the backside of Manhattan, which had no one architect, no single state of mind, but which grew out of earth like an eruption from the unconscious of multitudes, or the final elevation of the Underworld to the top of things. Up near the Cloisters. The Hudson slugged along at the base of the Harlem River and she always imagined that river on her right, and the East River on her left, because that's the way she and he entered Manhattan—from the top down; everything about their habitat seemed to involve being behind, in back of, off to the side, just because they began north in Maine.

Temple never showed any signs of affection towards Felicity. Her anxiety came from her familiarity with his mix of obsession and indifference. He wouldn't let up on her, but he wouldn't comfort her with one moment of human attention, either. Machines express pain even if they don't know it (that's why they make those noises) and Felicity surmised that Temple felt that same kind of pain. She had known him from childhood. At least since she was a teen and he was a young man, but she had known all about him way before they met. He summered in Maine and she lived there, a townie, as he would say. From day one the relationship was established between them. She waited for him to express the pain he was in, and he showed her his cold profile. Like a radar machine, he kept track of her moves, remaining himself isolate and invisible.

The movie theater smelled of bathroom, public bathroom, or the way cheap bars smell in the afternoon. Green ammonia. Temple sat straight as a chair in the aisle, chewing gum solemnly, his eyes narrowed. They were watching *Young At Heart* and already it was one of Felicity's favorite movies. Frank Sinatra expressed his pain with every move he made. Felicity and Temple had been to the same movie and had the same kind of conversation about money when she was a late teen. But she was the only one of the two of them that day who remembered the original occasion and how similar it felt to this one. She knew very little about him—only that he had stopped dealing drugs and was now engaged in something like real estate, so he was still rich. She had come to him for help as a last resort. Meantime an aura of disappointment floated about him, one of those emotions so powerful it swelled and deflated in the air.

Tears tickled Felicity's smile as she watched the movie. The story was innocent and she reminiscent. Suddenly she felt Temple gazing at her, the way they do when they're thinking about taking you to bed, and her blood rushed up her legs like a run in a stocking. She was horribly dressed in jeans, a sweatshirt, a leather jacket, gray and stained underwear, ripped socks, sneakers and a red baseball cap. But she still believed that happiness was chasing her and she was only just missing it by inches. She wore that look they have when they're trying to trick happiness into getting caught. Now it took the form of her thinking Temple would break down at last, be kind, and rescue Matty. She pretended to be unaware of his gaze, but her fingers nearly broke among themselves, and all because he was looking at her.

She stood up first when the movie was over, and rubbed her eyes with her fists. The blood in her limbs was still inaccurately flowing too close to her navel and crotch, and she stretched to a child's height beside him. Temple, still seated, put his hands up on her hips and hauled himself to his feet, sighing. His hair was both yellow and white. The nod in his head continued. He was exceedingly handsome in an Anglo-Saxon way. For someone with a bullet still lodged in his bottom, he looked remarkably sporty. Like a prep school teacher. He had the smile of a know-it-all, the kind that automatically lowers the self-esteem of its witness. Felicity looked at the gummy floor under her feet and followed him out to the sun.

Let's go to the Cork House, he said. I'll buy you lunch.

She trailed him down the thickly shadowed street. Litter and stone. No animals. No birds. The stones smelled of lots of foods, beef, fish, bread, chocolate, those natural resources which the stony streets themselves lacked. The Cork House had a plastic green shamrock hanging over its double doors. Felicity slipped ahead of him inside. It was a family restaurant and bar with four televisions, one in each corner, and a bathroom which was always out of toilet paper. She knew the place well and was reassured by its lack of progress.

He ordered the food but when he talked to her he seemed to talk to the television. He didn't look at anyone while he spoke, but always stared over their shoulder as if conjuring up another, imaginary, and better listener. He was, she realized, more sensitive about himself than usual, and lacking in a shared humor. When he laughed, it was his secret why. But she blocked out her anxiety, flirting over the lip of her beer, and telling him her terrible story with the eyes of a beggar. How many hospitals, clinics and doctors she had visited, trying to get help for her daughter, and how they all said the same thing. Since she had no health insurance, she would be at the bottom of a donor's list, and her daughter would probably not survive the wait.

I can get you a liver, he said, but you realize it's illegal. You have to bring your kid to a clinic on the border—it's really a small hospital—where a surgeon will do it. You won't need to be there or have anything to do with the actual operation. Okay? He's perfectly qualified. He just can't get a license to practice here.

I don't have a cent to my name.

Well, I know that.

So?

I'll give you something to do, don't worry. I can use your help.

How will I get her to the hospital?

A friend will do all that.

She'll be scared if I don't go too.

I wouldn't look a gift horse in the mouth.

Well, what do you want me to do?

Deliver something to someone.

Don't tell me what it is.

Don't worry. Here's the food. Eat.

As long as you swear the doctor isn't a quack.

I swear.

I'll do anything, she said.

He liked that comment and became almost seductive while she mopped up ketchup with her fries. He wiped a red drop from her lip with his napkin, then pressed the spot to his own mouth. He ordered her a Bloody Mary. He drank from it too, sipping from the wet area she had used. He put his hand on her leg, and they reminisced about the backside of Manhattan ten years before, when Temple chased a lover of hers out of her apartment on Avenue D with a can of mace.

I'm glad to see you are learning to live alone, said Temple. You act like you've got a sign hanging on you reading GO AWAY. Why's that?

I guess my willpower is on low. I can't do much more than worry about Matty, my daughter, the sick one. I really only care about my kids. These days.

That's good. As it should be.

Yeah?

But I bet you drink too much.

For what?

For your health.

Uch, so?

I bet you still like sex though, right?

I don't think about it, I told you.

I don't believe you.

Well, it's the truth.

Want to go to a motel for the rest of the day?

What for?

For fun. We can go to the Tower.

Wow, that would be a laugh and a half.

The Tower Motel was a pink building that peeked at the Hudson through a lot of steel and concrete. It was set back blushing off the street, and was a notorious place for illicit sex, drug deals and gambling. The pink and green room smelled like the inside of a nose, Felicity said, holding her own between her fingers. The bedspread was frayed and dimpled, the sheets soft with age. He had brought her some ready-made Bloody Marys from a liquor store en route, and she swilled one down, hating herself the way she did every time she drank out of need and not out of pleasure. He said from his back on the bed, I never met a junkie or a drunk who liked themselves, or their habit.

You really think I'm a drunk? she asked.

Never mind what I think. Get over here.

She climbed in beside him and buckled up her knees while she trembled.

Are you safe? he asked.

From you?

You know what I mean.

I take the pill.

Did you want to get pregnant when you did?

Uh huh. Being a mother was the best choice I ever made.

Well, you sure didn't like the father much. You want to marry again?

Never, ever, ever, not ever, NEVER.

Why not?

I already told you I promised God, when I was in that halfway place, that I would never marry again, if I could just survive the first one.

And I told you that was a dangerous promise.

Well, I meant it.

And whatever the case, you got rid of Hugo.

No, you did.

You set it up.

I was scared.

Yeah, but you're fucked up. You give with one hand and take with the other. You send out mixed signals. It's all for attention, or so you can look good, or maybe you're just confused. But I'm not dumb. I know that I serve the function of Bad Guy for you, so you can have a clear conscience.

That's not a very nice thing to say. Besides, you seem to like doing these things.

I do. It's true.

But you don't even care about me.

I must care if I like to see you suffer.

Shit.

Stop shaking and get out of bed. I don't want to sleep with you. You're too old, too used, too motherly for my taste.

She jumped from the bed and ran to the bathroom with her clothes in her arms. Awkwardly she dressed, her fingers fumbling with zippers and buttons. She even put her hat back on before she returned to the room where he lay. She stood over him, questioning.

Why did we end up so much on the edge of society, Temple? Others, our neighbors, did okay.

There's this theory I've got—of circles. Rings. Tracks. Whatever you want to call them. Everybody occupies space in one of these closed circuits. The Mafia and the Kennedys are together in one of them whether they like it or not, because they both have the same degree of power and money. Frank Sinatra's in that one too. Then there are little tight rings—where people are so rich they're free of all thoughts of money and power. Royalty, dictators, certain movie stars. However, the larger the rings, containing more and more people, the less power and money is involved, people become anonymous. Those were our neighbors, the middle class, or the middle circle. It's a circus, for Christ's sake. . . . But you and I are in the waste dump—or not quite—the homeless and crazy are in that one, picking up garbage, the throw-aways getting the throwaways. You and I are just on the edge of that one, no matter how much money we have. It's not a very big space where we are, but it's got a lot of people crammed into it—rejects, criminals, ones who didn't quite qualify for power or for anonymity. I should've qualified, but I didn't like the people in there, my people, my family's friends.

Felicity said, Sounds like circles of evil. Where do nuns and priests go?

You're right. They have their own little crystal ball.

Is our circle totally debased?

Totally, though I don't worship Satan or anything like that. I just maintain a position of secrecy while I do what I have to do. What I really turned away from was notoriety.

You might recall that I used to have some measure of fame?

Sure. I worked in your campaign. You gave these great speeches on civil rights and the Constitution.

Good, you remember. I'm still a committed American.

Yeah, really. Are you happy now in this trap, track?

No way. No one is content in the one they're in. That's the race. The sting. The bite. The kill. I want to be in the one above the Kennedys and they do too.

Is it progress to move from one to the next?

I don't believe in progress. Can't you see? That's the whole point of the picture. They're traps. They go nowhere. They're not hierarchies.

He tossed back the sheets then, exposing his hairy legs and polka-dotted shorts. His chest hair was silver. He looked as if he had never let his body see the sun. As he dressed, he spoke to her formally.

Here's what you've got to do. Go to Boston for about a month. I have a friend who can find you a place to stay. Wait there till I contact you.

But the kids?

They can stay with you.

They're already registered in a school there.

I know. So continue to bring them.

Then what?

I'll set you up with a person down on the border. You'll switch your daughter with the package I mentioned. It'll all take place near a small private airstrip outside Calexico. You've probably never seen a landscape like that one. You'll stay in a motel that's located right next to the only ranch in the area. A gal will pick you up soon to take your kid to the clinic. She'll also give you the instructions. Her name is Mona. I hate that name. She's my slave. I call her Money instead.

If she's your slave, I guess you can call her anything you want, said Felicity.

Felicity, you are now my slave too.

Sure, she laughed.

Now here's some cash for your trip. And here's the name of the contact in Boston.

I'm not too happy with this. It scares me.

Why so? You've got a master now, said Temple with a tight smile and his head nodding as if he was riding the subway downtown. You always wanted a master. Many women do.

Don't say that.

It's true, he insisted.

Women have to have men friends in order to survive in this world. That's not slavery. That's survival.

Oh? Think about it. Hope I'll marry you someday? You used to.

No.

Why not? That hurts my feelings.

Come on, Temple, don't play with me.

Years ago I promised you I would always watch out for you. I keep those promises. I also told you that you will belong to me sooner or later, remember? You loved it. You thought it was romantic.

Okay, but now I hate the thought. I told you I hate marriage. More than anything.

Only because it brings reality to the surface. Bondage.

That's right, she said.

But you're already in bondage. Why not get the benefits?

I'm not in bondage. Why do you say that? I live alone.

You yearn. You still yearn.

And what about you, Temple? What happened to you? Why have you gotten so mean?

I was always mean. Now do everything I said, he called. If you want to save your daughter's life.

Can anyone be saved by someone evil? Tom asked.

She had no answer. He noted that she carried around a peculiar collection of books—Trotsky, Baudelaire, *Field Guide to Western Birds*, woodworking, *Wuthering Heights*. She never let her children out of her sight or mentioned their father. Her own father was part Eskimo, and drifted down into Maine where he worked as a logger and was tended by a small band of misfit women, all alcoholic and part Italian and Sachem Indian (offspring of the same anarchists who came to make marble gravestones in New Hampshire, and were chased into obscurity by the FBI and were the forefathers of Tom's people.) The anarchist tradition continued in this matriarchal tribe. She had a happy childhood, given gulps of Southern Comfort by loving women. Her father pushed her on timber downriver in the warm summer weather. The smell of lilacs in the spring and newly poured tar were sensations which sent her into maddened memories of early youth. Sometimes she longed for home, but feared to return since all but one of the adults (a cranky aunt) had been carried away by bad livers and heart attacks.

One summer she met Temple on the lake which lay near the river. He was laying back in a canoe, stripped down to the waist, his skin reddish brown from the sun and his hair bleached nearly white. She had heard about him—a rich teen, from a house on a hill, with no parents, both had died, and only an uncle to care for him. By mistake she saw him sucking his thumb, alone in the canoe, his face turned up to the sun. The gesture was both pathetic and arousing. She was embarrassed and turned her face to the water. She was sixteen years old, and fishing. She looked twelve, his favorite age for girls. He was said to be spoiled (even if orphaned), suspicious, ambitious and afraid of fully developed females. He paddled over to the riverbank where Felicity was nested on rocks among leaves and took her for a slow float around the lake. Her body was like a kid's and she wore a red cap with a visor to shade her eyes. He eyed her with adoration and desire, while she flopped around, rocking the boat and sticking her bare legs into the water. He imagined her as hairless as a baby, except where the black hair poured out from under her cap and her eyebrows and eyelashes were thick and expressive on her face. And he wrestled with her in the canoe, she was laughing hysterically because every touch felt like a tickle, until the canoe tipped over and they fell into the water. Then the way he grabbed her between her legs made her realize he wasn't just fooling around, and she pulled away and swam to shore, panicky and panting, while he swam after her, dragging the canoe along with him. She ran through the woods, home, but she was hooked on him, his hand had been like a hook in the privacy of her groin, and she spent the rest of that summer dragging around after him. He for his part had no desire for her, since he discovered, with his hand, that she was not prepubescent, but he savored her childlike appearance nonetheless, and admired her lack of education and security, and she became his sidekick, his Sancho Panza, his Tonto, his good luck charm for a couple of summers following.

Felicity for her part never wanted to grow up and understood that he didn't want her to, either. She understood it with her body and her psyche and not with her mind. His hand had let her know he was judging her as she judged herself. How could she not, therefore, be stuck on him?

One night at the ocean place when I was pregnant I trudged across shells and stones in the night with the water sloshing on my sneakers, and I looked up and saw the lights from a little saltbox, all yellow and gentle, and for a few minutes I wanted that kind of security. It looked so good! But I guess I'm just a hobo by nature. What can you do if you are what you are? I'm not like some of us who are thrown out like trash and don't want to be. They want the little yellow lights and what goes along with them. They want a roof and a root to correspond. So let them have it. They didn't ask to be born. We have to take care of each other's needs. I don't happen to have that need, but I do have some. For my kids mostly. Am I really the only one in the world who loves them?

That's scary, and why I gotta get settled. Later, I can walk for miles, get high, right? Getting high is getting free.

Not really, said Tom. Then he felt ashamed and added: My job seems to be to shoot you down.

My job, said Felicity, is to believe in everything.

Five

An American spoke Spanish to a Mexican waiter who replied in English. There were lots of doors leading in. Geraniums grew along the edge of the gravel parking lot. They circled the doors, about twenty of them, and found themselves crossing a brick tile terrace where there were green chairs and tables and trellises spangled with Christmas lights. A little bar, a man. Delicate pink flowers fell from watery wine glasses. Calla lilies bloomed along a stone esplanade which faced the sea. There was a wrought iron balcony over each door and pink fans of linen stuffed in every glass on every table. A Mayan tin sun shone on the pink stucco wall. Felicity had put the children out on the sand to play and now she stood behind Tom on the other side of the wall. He asked her what it was like to be pregnant.

Why, what for? she asked.

It's a question I always wanted to ask someone.

I'll tell you about the time I was pregnant with Lee, because then I was happy—alone—near the sea.

As with a great storm or onset, she could hear through the walls of her body the hysteria of two whose voices hit a pitch neither male nor female. Getting pregnant only took those noises and an interior silence, a moment which she knew every time. Age-old urge, emergency among the whirlpools, the fragments and sweeping curves of her torso. A sudden squall, the flutter of a breeze in her ear, and she was done.

She began to harden with the first baby. A firm heel slid across the palm of her hand, under her navel, now like a moonsnail with a cat's eye at its apex. Her wastes, and the baby's, moved in opposite directions from the nutrients. Her breasts tightened to tips of pain. She entered her psyche daily on rising, and like Saint Clare who sucked the breast of Saint Francis, she frenziedly inhaled the Ave Maria. A she dwelled inside, in fact. An expedition of several oar ships.

Perfumes of the senses met a collection of bones and springs, and in her genitals a language of body fluids and secretions, tracts and tissues, bone marrow, breast milk, joint fluids—she had to think of these. The creation could only read itself!

The embryo went to sleep early one night and in the liquidy darkness I stepped down the center of the road, by day bustling with cars and tourists. I walked towards the point which circled back along a harbor into town. I took a westerly direction, knowing the sea would always have the last word.

This is the way to see a place—looking from darkness into lighted rooms. So the fetus derives nourishment from the light of oxygen. The white clapboard houses conformed like little teakettles or mausoleums, with a staircase down the center, a kitchen beyond, and on either side a living room and study. The walls were marked with pictures of schooners and portraits of seafaring men. Streamlined launchers too, but no tramp steamers red with rust, no broad tugs, ropes, cables, or snakelike tubes winding from tanks; these were class ships. At twelve weeks the uterus is stretched like a canvas, larger than the pelvic cavity. It can be palpated above the symphysis pubis. But these rooms were white with polished wood. The furniture was stiff and economical. Like the ships themselves, they equated tidiness with worth. Old

*women dusted and drifted through the mannish spaces, giving to
them the otherworldly sheen of sisters from the last century.*

*She was often sick, either hunched up or bent over, retching
into a toilet bowl. Nature is extravagant. Her body was a difficulty in much the same spirit that a person's gender or income can
be under certain conditions. Inside her eyes she saw placenta,
membranes, amniotic fluids, cervical cul-de-sacs, a vulva and an
interior like the gums of an infant. However, her mental dimen-
sions tipped towards the metaphysical. G-d had been forced out of
just such a world. She trudged up and down the island and daily
visited beaches which were duneless but sided by slick streaks of
beachgrass. The shadows of seagulls spilled along water's edges.
Silk pennants fluttered over the breakwater and sometimes rain
glistened in the dark. Fishing boats and cutters had black-green
barnacled bottoms. The ruin of the deck and upper structures of
many ships looked like fruit picked by sharks. Every stay and
handrail held a bird in the dawn. Sticky oil, belched from a tunnel, had birds stuck on their pin-like toes. The poop went down,
the bow went up, it was her body walking and a teeny skeleton
inside like a cabin.*

*On the strand the waves were disorganized, they champed and
struck each other, currents tugging at a mash of pebbles. Few
shells, and those were cracked scallops or an old horseshoe crab. A
flotsam of styrofoam and plastic baggies. God's grave is blue and
above. When you are living on the edge of your society are you
closer to the center of the next era? If there was such a quality as
human nature, she now had to assume it was grounded in the
machine she inhabited and which, again, inhabited her. The
vagina and cervix in pregnancy are blue to purple. She was sure
drug therapy was the best cure for depression. Motion was libera-
tion from the gross inertia of the body which held swellings small
as berries and full of air. You could be healed by leaping in the sea*

which is why she gravitated towards water towns. There flowering seaweed cooled her sore feet. The surface oysters with pearls embedded in pink flesh made her feel like a link of woman, coral to red, nameless as a breast. Now a hint of autumn let her spirits rise, her mind race.

I don't want to be a king or captain or bishop or chair. A summer of record-breaking heat and humidity created a swimming pollution, humans gasped like fish. In the seas a scandal of unsanitary objects. While five thousand small herrings nested in the stomach of a sperm whale and each one of them contained crabs who in turn had eaten algae, night storms kept the beaches lined with silver wiggling krill and human feces. The air stayed dense and dirty as if the rain itself had been a form of excretion. Birth is a calamity. So I cling to my infant and it to me.

I have become unified with my materials. Thorns made the beard of Jesus what it was. No field of blue flowers. No matter what I touch or work on, it's only me touching or working. Conversion is not putting on something new but shedding something old.

In her first pregnancy she found herself finally focussed on the presence of her body. Nothing was distracting from the fact that the mucus of the cervix is less viscid than sputum. She was conscious of how mechanistic and unnecessary a human life really was; every fact was an affirmation of perdition. Rich and poor women look stark but strong. Clapboard houses, low to the ground, with protuberant fans and television antennae nestled in shrubbery lusciously green and dotted with flowers. Petunias, limp, with purple trumpets too, proliferated. Some gardens had salmon-pink borders of impatiens and on the roadsides the clover was ripe, a farm was for sale, fresh baked pies were lined up on planks beside beach plum jelly and apple cinnamon. Mopeds and bikes cruised the narrow roads where she crawled. Pastures humped under her back in the long grass, the sky was often misty or gray. She wondered, when she woke out there one day, if the objects she saw on the left in her dreams were emanating from that side of her brain.

Well, I said, you sweep people away like a dream. I'm glad when you call to me, Let's go. Seeking face. I WILL seek your face.

Is it human nature to crave the love of indifferent people? Does a displaced center become a periphery? She certainly did, even while she sustained bonds to distant friends. Past their shoulders she always seemed to glimpse the image of someone who had for-gotten she was alive, and hardly cared to discover she was. One such person told her that the mirror for human nature was art and that the secret therefore of her essence could be found in the recog-nition she would feel before certain words and works. Without such recognition she could only feel revulsion towards the experi-ence of producing more body fluids, another epiglottis, en-dometrium, and so on.

Pregnancy created a tie to her own accidental source. To view the condition as a disease which she had caught was to reject the knowledge of a human for its own nature. A plant might look like it's growing a beard, but anyone knows that it isn't, since each form can only reproduce itself.

She didn't remain as static as a plumed worm—building its home in a papery tube. A trumpet worm constructs a permanent home from a golden cone in the sand.

She inhabited her inhabitant and kept on moving. The larvae of soft-shell clams do no less. In an environment that changes wildly, creation creates a lot of itself. In a fierce storm barnacles, worms, and mussels reproduce in droves. If she wondered who re-ally owned her hand, writing with a pen, and where she could be located, she now knew one thing at least and for the time being: she was present at her own life.

The collar-like erection on the beach was made by a moonsnail to protect her eggs. So she was an organism which existed alongside the other particulars in the universe. She was really here where the egg cases of skates, called "mermaid purses," are dry and black with two spiny tendrils at either end.

By accepting the fact of her existence she had to accept the terms in which science generally spoke of such facts. Herring gulls eat horseshoe crabs, but she turned away from the temptation of brutalism. She, like some, tried to believe that the secret name of the power that is the foreginning of everything was HUMAN. While the integrity of her pregnancy was maintained by high levels of estrogen and progesterone, her personal integrity was maintained by identifying with eremites.

She had begun to feel close to the ground. The poverty line was dollars above her, she who had been one of the working poor. America ran through her sleep too fast. But beach heather with its yellow spring blossoms was not her bed either. Grasshoppers belong to beach grass.

One morning a cloud bank slipped over the island like a smoker trailing around a garden. Seaweed in the cracks of rock and bits of sponge and seaside goldenrod held her, lying in the sun. The trees were filmy, the national shades of noon still softened by immortal light. A caterpillar here, a snake there, by Labor Day most of the wildflowers were eliminated. Small baggy areas formed in the troughs between dunes, and she hid in them with a stolen apple pie. To be happy alone you don't need to be a martyr.

From some leaves thick as leather hung nuts, rocky brown ones with dimpled caps. Beach peas grew in the sand with wild cherry and beach plum. I'd eat kelp, sea lettuce, maybe even Irish moss. I didn't want to hitchhike at my age or in my condition; instead I scuffed my sneakers through the sandy soil and twitched with the pains in my calves. Pork of veal, pork of veal, someone called in a room through the trees. The light seemed painted on the surface of each oak leaf. So I remembered artifice, I a free woman who had neither home nor office, and then I saw my husband coming, and wept.

Six

Tom shut Felicity down the minute he sensed that her story was on a down-curve. Don't get sentimental with me, he warned, but she promised she would stick to facts if he would just listen to her. "I'm in some kind of peril," she confessed. And in the hotel, when the children were sleeping, she hid behind the drapes, pressed up against the window and talked, while he stood, hands folded in front of his groin and head tipped down like one waiting in line for the Eucharist.

"Before I went to New York or met you, I traveled down here with the kids. Matty was really sick then. Between her illness and rejections from hospital officials, I could hardly get up in the morning. We moved back and forth along the border."

Crossed over. Squat palm trees with fanning leaves, a sandy soil, small adobe houses, wine red bougainvillea like paper, like velvet, graffiti of human faces on a cement wall, chickens nipping at nothing, and jacaranda trees as blue as lilac. There the people were thick, short and brown like her. They were like her brothers and sisters. When the earth trembled, there was an accompaniment of sound-rolling rocks, a thunder under the soil. She remembered Hades coming up from the Underworld near the red flowers with all that clatter. He pulled Persephone down but she held her daughter tighter to her. Pomegranates grew wild and red as peppers, and their seeds spilled from the pouches to feed the insects. They say that the songs of birds make fruits grow ripe. Honeysuckle thickened with fragrance outside a wall.

We slept outside. To our right was the sea; it always used to be at my left. I saw by the cactus that not only was all this land covered by water but that air itself is just a lighter form of water that we live in. Mountain lions are still being hunted down in the Sierras, it's late, but they survive. Like all of us they spend their lives on consumption, for time is food.

Felicity looked for a home in the papers:

WANTED—HOUSE DESPERATELY.
Bank foreclosed homes
Free list of repossessed condos
Darling, immaculate, delinquent property
Government homes
$ (you repair)
By owner. FHA assumable
Mobile home, adult recreational park
Need a down payment?
Carefree condo
If I can't find it, it doesn't exist!

My indecision about Matty was a plague. I didn't want to go near Temple for help again, I wanted to be free. But I was living on last dimes and her increasing illness. I went to lots of churches and prayed to Mary. But every time I started a novena, I would forget in the middle and ruin it. So no wonder they didn't work! I learned a lot from books, too, that we got from the public libraries. The kids and I would read about history and geography. We wanted to know where we were in the world.

Montezuma ruled like a divinity. Ancestral hierarchies were rampant. Many of them, even in the Americas, were derived from ties to Rome and the Church.

Matty broke my heart. I blamed myself for all the drink and smoke and went on drinking and smoking. Decisions are like climbing up a ladder into space. I didn't know how to make one. The only way to feel safe in space is by holding a baby. They take care of their mothers. Try it. Hold one someday. I hated my body in those days because I blamed it for her sickness, and then I felt nothing for anyone, not even myself. I was my own enemy. Hateful.

I felt no desire outside the desire for a miracle. If someone good would only save us.

The land had belonged to the Comanches and I was one of them. By 1830 Anglos outnumbered Mexicans along the border. Most were Catholic who despised Indians and Mexicans. Four to one. A serious problem for them was slavery, and why not? Mexico outlawed slavery in 1822. And they didn't want any more Americans coming in. Slavery meant disaster because slaves had so many children. Texas died for the freedom to keep slaves. Have slaves or die. Temple too might die for such freedom.

In 1840 Nuevo Leon and Coahuila tried to secede from Mexico.

A Republic of the Rio Grande was declared with Laredo as its capital. It produced one hero—Antonio Zapata whose head was chopped off and pickled in brandy.

I don't want to be anything like a man.

The Taiwanese have set up offices in the US where they regulate business in the Maquiladoras. *Vámanos,* said the Mexican people and headed off to work, from onions to sugar beets to pickles to cherry trees to strawberry fields to peaches and the asparagus fields. The two borders—Cali and Mexi, Mexicali and Calexico. Sex confuses citizenship, and family trees take root in the river. Power to the people.

She ran out of money and hid in an orphanage, helping some nuns take care of abandoned children. There she learned how to organize large groups of people—how to build cubbies and line up the food—how to make shoes look neat in a row and how to put privacy and silence into practice. She learned how to be efficient under pressure, and how to live in a community. Matty however was getting sicker and the nuns urged Felicity to return to get help in America. In that sandy soil the flowers were sometimes brown, like orchids and irises and the streaks in pansies, and sometimes sexual in intent: desert flowers with rubbery ridges and frills gape up hungrily at the sky. They look like they were born to suck. Sometimes Felicity thought she saw them contract, curl in; they were colored yellow and salmon pink. She thought of all the orphans turned out onto the streets at age twelve when they lost the orange glow of health and grew ragged; she thought of the children north of the border who were in detention homes and gangs. She travelled to Children's Hospital in Boston, where again she was given small hope of an organ donor for Matty, especially when they were penniless, and she looked for Temple from there. He made the connections and she headed back to Boston and Tom, then South again with her daughters, according to his directions.

About a hundred miles east of San Diego, and a mile north of the border, she travelled under the influence of Mona, who liked to call herself Money, too. She was a transvestite who worked in a club on the Mexican side of the border "giving head," as she said, to the white college kids who came down for the weekends. She wore silk stockings and silk skirts and shirts and smoked cigarillos. In a pouch under her shirt she carried money and drugs. She met Felicity and the girls at the E-Z 8 Motel; she was carrying a box of candy in either hand. Red and gold lettering on both covers and crinkly chocolate cups inside. Except one—the left one—was not chocolate and Felicity was being sent to San Diego to deliver it to a man working for the the border patrol. The other box she gave to Matty who began pinching each candy in search of caramel.

The hard square ones are always the caramels, Money told Matty, then noted: She looks Mestiza.

She is. All mixed-up. They both are.

Don't be nervous. I'll take care of her. Good care. Temple told me to. I do whatever he says and more.

Is he your pimp or something?

No way! Money laughed. He's my master. I'm his slave-girl. I do anything he wants. It makes me happier than it makes him.

In what way?

It keeps me alive.

She plucked at her elastic panties to show they were too tight and sauntered up to the oval mirror which was only as clear as wax paper. Leaning forward she scrutinized her lips, her teeth. She was smooth-skinned and pretty, with soft dark hair and large man-made breasts. Her features were Mexican, her expression melancholy.

I'll see you back here in about twenty-four hours, she told Felicity. Just sit tight and see the sights. Your girl will come back. She just needs a checkup, no big deal.

Matty rested her face against her mother's leg, her eyelids seemed weighted down by her heavy black eyelashes. Her color was jaundiced. Felicity stirred up her hair.

Why can't I go too? she demanded in a rude tone.

Be serious, said Money. This is not exactly aboveboard.

What we're doing.

How so?

No, you wouldn't want to know. The best thing is to just accept it as a gift from Temple and do your job for him, whatever it is. This way he'll be good to you and that'll be that.

And what happens if I don't do it?

He'll—I don't know, said Money with a shrug. You know him longer than I do. Come on, *chica*, let's go.

Matty buckled and cried, following Money into the heat, with her body twisted up like a question mark. Felicity grabbed Lee's hand and dragged her down the street, after them, but at a distance. She was crying. The yellow ground was hard as a rock, though there was no rock material in it that she could see. Felicity was talking to Jesus: "I thought you were the shepherd who left behind the ninety-nine sheep who were safe. You went out and searched for the one who was lost, remember? You were happy when you found it, since ninety-nine is a number that comes with the left hand, and you liked everything weighing in in the right hand. . . Remember?"

Crowds collected as she and the little girl progressed, and the streets began to thicken with commerce. Faces watched her weeping and walking and talking. Neon pagodas in the paved and pitted roads, lemonade and cigarettes, tacos in curbside braziers; she saw a guitar warped by grease drippings, and a man's hand on it. She smelled banana leaf tamales and bought herself a beer. She saw Money and Matty climb in a cab and she plunged forward after them. Hidalgo ceramics and Saltillo blankets lined the road, alongside toy violins, leather vests, chess sets made of malachite, piñatas and whips. Awnings, vending stalls, corrugated metal, tons of people. Some spoke English, some Spanish.

Felicity screamed Matty, and ran after the cab to pull her back out and take her away.

She got as far as the window and looked in as it moved away. Matty was looking down at her hands. Felicity could tell that Money had given her more of the goat's-milk caramels, and the child had chocolate dribbles on her chin, streaks of dust down the lines of her tears. Felicity's crying was by then a moan or a buzz in the back of her throat. Something ripped from the spirit is far more painful than something ripped from the skin, though I wouldn't want to test this hypothesis. At least I can swear an action does occur, and it makes me very sore. To say goodbye is sad enough when you can be sure the other will return. When that hope is fretted with un-certainty, the whole air is transformed and the strange thing is, you are the only one who knows it!

I don't own any of this. None of it belongs to me. Not the television or what's playing on it. Not the Gideon Bible. Not the road, the car, the dust or the movie playing down the road. I exist separate from all that, for the children of the

Lord are like his fragrance, since they have fallen from the grace of the beginning, and still carry that grace and that fragrance in their mouths and ears and nostrils. They hold it in their hands. It lies in the light on their faces and in the darkness of their closed hands, and in their sleep.

The delivery of the chocolate box was unmemorable. I just handed it over to some big half-naked border cop at the door of a bungalow in Southeast San Diego, and then drove away. I sensed that this was only the beginning of my side of the bargain. Ficus and bougainvillea colored up the sunny alley alongside the bungalow and clashed with a tomato-red Porsche parked there. Almost immediately I returned to the original motel with Lee. We lay in bed together watching t.v. and only went on the hot streets to get Zingers and Royal Crown Cola. The air was actually white. I didn't like being anywhere. I thought my guts would explode with the acid of my anxiety. If I hadn't had Lee to nuzzle up to, I would've collapsed. She played with her sister's toy soldiers. The room was like a battlefield rebuilt from World War II—cheap plastic khaki-colored soldiers hung off the bedspread, the plastic plant, the television wires. She went pow-pow and knocked them down, pretending to be Matty, then climbed into my arms before returning to the kill. I told her war was obsolete. I told her patriotism was an archaic concept. Once I explained what the words meant, and she understood, she asked, "Does that mean I can start playing with girl's stuff now?"

The day Matty was meant to come back, it rained and she didn't. The sky was murky, yellow, warm. I watched Lee's every move. Her smooth brown shoulders, the wings of her shoulder blades, her long shadowy spine, they made me smile proudly on the one hand and cry on the other. I didn't know which I loved better, her body or my love for her body. It takes years to come to trust the cars and curbs and sharp corners, to let your children move ahead of you, while your head is turned. Oh years. I had no idea, not one, of what was happening to my daughter whom I had watched over hour by hour, since her birth. It is impossible to describe the anxiety of those hours, now, spent with her out of sight. I stared into the television and then outside the window. Across the dirt road in a bar the *putas* sipped lemonade and leaned against their windows too.

In the evening a woman with man's legs brought me a letter from Temple, saying Matty was fine but needed another day to complete the tests. "We were unrealistic," he wrote, "about the time it would take. You can stay in the motel and wait. I'll pay. And visit." I took Lee out for a drive along the border and back to the motel where Money was waiting with tickets for an outdoor fair. I was not invited to go along, but watched her go off with Lee, anxiously. It was of course a set up because I wasn't alone five minutes before Temple appeared. I was not happy to see his face. He looked out of place in the west, even though he was wearing a string tie and a cowboy hat. He brought tequila and chips and salsa into my room and shook up margaritas while I sat under the bedspread, resisting both questions and alcohol. I thought he might have bad

news, but he said don't worry, your kid is doing fine. Great.
She'll get what she needs. In a matter of weeks I'm sure we
can do the transplant. Drink. I took the glass and felt the heat
of alcohol in my thighs and groin and upper arms, a toxin.
Temple was as usual estranged from everything around him.
He was present but indifferent. He stood by the television
where he kept all the drink and chips and stared vacantly at
the wall. He told me what he wanted me to do next. I felt my
hair grow tight in my skull and heavy. I lifted it with my
hands and laughed. No way! But he said I'm not kidding.
Come on, Temple, I don't do that stuff, I told him and he
said, I know, it's time you did. But what if I don't want to? I
asked. That'll make it better for me, he answered.

I wouldn't do it, she told Tom. There are some things. You
just don't do. I mean. I'm not going to tell you what either,
because you're kind of innocent.

So what did he do then?

Well, obviously he didn't kill me. He left, for a short time.
He still called me his slave.

You're right. This is a story I don't want to hear.

Seven

They sat up over the Avenidad Revolución, looking down on people's heads. They drank beer. The children had Cokes and hung over the stall-like balcony beside them. Tourists streamed by, pausing to examine the rugs and ceramics lined up on the sidewalks. The sun lay on Tom's face like a white-gloved hand, and he felt nauseous. Looking at her sideways, he couldn't stop wondering what Temple wanted her to do and what she finally didn't do. Stories can be stranger than experience. They can impart a sensation as heavy as morning breath. Sometimes women seemed profoundly impure to Tom—murky as an old lake. "When you swim in one, you don't know what you will brush against, what will bristle against your skin. At the same time, the cool and refreshing quality that the swim provides—there's nothing like it. Women are deeper and kinder than men, but I don't like the passage sometimes through those tender depths of theirs. It scares me. It can even sicken me." At that moment Felicity sickened him—or her story did, in a context of nihilism and commerce. He told her he wanted to walk back across the border before she could start up one of her stories again. The children had begun to warm up to him as he grew aware of the subtle differences between them, and their potentials for intelligence and gifts of music, math, politics. They equally began to warm up to him—laughing, telling jokes, holding his hands. Someone thought they were a family and told Matty to get their father to buy them a ceramic Mickey Mouse. The sky was a high gray color. Ghost color.

107

Back in their room, the girls lay down on the floor to watch t.v. Felicity meanwhile crawled under the bed to look for a shoe and stayed there plucking at the springs and talking so Tom couldn't see her. This time he placed himself against the drapes and stared out the window; the shadowy belly of a plane crossed over the room.

Temple came back and said he wanted to go for a drive. To show me hills I'd never seen the likes of before. I said I'd only go if he didn't make me do anything I didn't want to. He agreed but asked me one thing. What? To pretend to be his slave. Just for the duration of the day, the drive. Better a slave than your wife, I agreed, but he reminded me that in my own eyes they were nearly the same. He had a rent-a-car which was all white.

There's a panic in the noonday hour, in love's demise, no "controls." Over and over the wonder of wounds from human deceptions returns, the mind can't top off, or regulate its notions, and all emotions won't be stalled, but will roll and roll, backwards and forwards.

The car climbed over the mountain to see what it could see.

It shows you're not in love with me, if you could make me marry someone you're not in love with yourself.

He hates to think like this.

See that grass and the pretty bosom in it? I think that's strange.

A woman and her mother.

The highway's wet after yesterday's rain.

I can't recall who told me to be good to please myself, every time I make a bed.

And I'm not in love with her, not because she's a woman, but I don't want to marry anyone I don't really know.

Some people want to feel passion all the time, or do, and even dream about being adored, and adoring, in order to feel engorged.

Sunday is morning's obstruction.

I was mean to my child. Slapped her chest. She followed me once too often. The room, a kitchen, shuffled with shock absorbing sounds; the wings of heaven were palpitating at the cruelty of that act.

Such mad mornings when everyone is crying and furious, and no longer curious.

Green light on the colorless grass.

Flattened out, ironing cloud.

Trees, no leaves, pulled up by the wires.

He doesn't really want to make her get married to someone she doesn't know, but deep down only just wants to get rid of her.

The wrath of a man like this comes on as a muted whirl, west, or east, to another "girl."

Wedlock has no key; but matrimony is too often locked around matters of money.

I pitched my tent in a nest of thistles, by the side of Baja. The black asphalt, like the Nile, carried traffic to my left, easterly, and I sat in a field of scratched grass.

A car looks like the wind, if you could see it.

See the woman, and her master, there. One unstraps the other's bra. A comely bosom in the bushes. A prune-blue nipple points North.

I wonder who will vomit, from too much driving. This woman or that man.

He says it's never too late to mend a rip; but don't hang over the cloth, waiting. "Life is of good and evil woven."

He wants her to turn into a boy. He has a smashed quality, like there was a fist.

The car has settled, backwards, in a coppertone meadow, and the highway goes, mortal slope, down.

Turn round and round and seduce the first lady you see.

How can I convince you that the tapestry is full of holes, the earth's a carpet floating in space, and that hill, going up, is a loose thread?

Her master put her down in this field by the forest. He can't explain why he did such a thing, except he hints that he was really a good guy underneath it all.

She who has been given, says she has chosen, solitude.

We're near the head of the thread; bite it.

Let's have a picnic instead.

We'll never get home—up or down. It's the edge.

Say to him, me: "It reminds!" Say it.

We lay down on this bristly meadow that sloped down to the highway. Bracken like sea sponge. Tea-green stuff. Sucky stuff. Flowers like mouths and vaginas in the cactus. He was detached, and I was surprised to see his head flat on the ground, unmoving, almost placid. I kept thinking about him dying. He had seemed to die once, with me, when I was seventeen, and he was so drunk he didn't know what he was doing when he laid me, so to speak, under a hawthorne tree, using a slow hand and a lot of sweet talk to break me down. At the end he had let out a sigh which was like a rattle from a snake, a baby, and a dying man. All in one. I figured that this was a good time to tell Temple that he had definitely deteriorated over the years from being a reasonably screwed-up individual, who was spoiled but troubled by things, to being that same individual without a conscience. I decided to tell him that he was, in a word, insane. He listened with an absorbing attitude, then took my hand and talked about body parts and how the human being is no greater than a machine with interchangeable parts. Livers, kidneys, hearts, tongues, penises, feet—he drew a picture of robotic reality, a take apart toy, where the mind or the emotions were gaseous emissions from the machinery. He kept saying, If you could just understand, you'd see it my way.

Never, I told him. I'm a mother. I just know I'm grateful to you for finding an organ for Matty. And it seems to me that this proves that there is such a thing as—well, unselfishness, or kindness—whatever you think of emotions.

Now you do sound like a wife, he said. I like that.

And then he went on with an accounting of populations around the world and what this meant. Forty million people will live in the United States by the turn of the century, most of them immigrants with too many children. I'm not being cold-blooded. Millions of children are starving already. Why have them? There must be a reason, there is a reason, he insisted.

Come on, stop talking about children in terms of reason. Either you recognize yourself in the world, or you don't, said Felicity.

Agreeably, he changed the subject and entered instead into a paranoid and pornographic account of women he had known, their body parts, and the disgust he felt at any woman over twelve.

"Men are cleaner. More honest in their builds. No secrets there. When we were just buying blood, it was much easier to persuade mothers that the money we gave them was equal to the blood. They didn't then try to find out everything about the organization, or snoop into my business. But after that, they got dangerous, the way they do, and talked too much, and asked too many questions, and changed their minds a million times. I couldn't trust one of them. If only they had acted the way you have—so far—with trust, silence, those qualities I associate with men, not women. But no. The female body is a manifestation of its meaning—secret, undisciplined, bloody."

Stop it. I want to go now, I told him.

He reeled to his feet and down the mountain with me following, and a lizard running before us, delicate in its bones and feet. My eyes sparked, and I wanted to drink or get high to transcend the world I was in. We went to a place called Hart's Chicken Parts which was smokey and packed with rednecks and truckers and whores. We drank without speaking, and he introduced me as his wife to anyone who cared to be interested. Then we weaved back to the motel down a highway saddened by the evening shadows.

Tom left her lying under the bed and began to watch the news on t.v. The girls were sleeping by then and he was not interested in any of them for that hour. She slipped out into the hall and onto the balcony and was gone long after he grew interested again. So he went and sought her out there. Planes rolled over them on air, and he yawned and groaned and caught scatterings of her news, while she dipped around like a shadow in the shadows.

I went out at night and whirled around in the light of the moon, a kind of dance in the marshes while the little continents between rushes of water squished underfoot and birds—dowitchers, plovers, godwits, curlews and one great blue heron—snoozed and cooed out of the dark. The watery sections were a dazzle of moon-mud or sapphire and when the train rushed through I danced for the conductor to see and saw him in return trying to understand. One night I came upon a woman awake, with two children, pruning a silver pear tree in her garden near the highway. Her children sat on her shoulders like the angels that flanked Mary. She told me she could find me a bench in a church to sleep on. But I told her kindly, no. The infamous sun would be up soon enough and I back at work. I wanted to dance the devil's dance in the dark till the water blued and the sky pinked. Then I'd go back where I came from. She was nice. She accepted me. Later I found out she was creating a happy commune smack on the border. It was twined with geraniums and laughter rang off the adobe walls. She believed that America was corrupting and all a kid needed was freedom from it to break his or her bad habit, and she wanted to save kids. She had a theory that prisoners should be released from jail and airlifted to other countries, dropped there, in the wilderness, not the city, and left to survive. It was what saved her husband. The world is one, but there is no center. The state is a myth, she said as laughter scattered red petals onto the bone dry ground, both sides of the wall. It is not a coincidence that all the walls and buildings are held together with sand. I thought she was like a saint, but when she gave me a pear to eat it lay heavy, cold and mineral in my hand. The fruit had turned into silver, which for all its beauty, horrified me. I have never met a real saint.

INFORMATION FELICITY GAVE TOM:

There is this man who does it by hand behind the supermarket.

The Nite Lite Motel is a good cheap motel, E-Z 8 another. Budget Beddy Bye stinks. The Mile of Cars is a nightmare.

She wanted to run away to Chula Vista, steal a horse and ride it to Coronado.

In El Centro there are fake farms, a desert atmosphere, and a detention camp for illegals; the broad margin includes them as they wait for immigration papers. To the west, at night, helicopters flash down floodlights and shoot into the under-brush; inside the helicopters are men whose people came to this country as immigrants.

In the *maquiladoras* are assembly lines operated at three dol-lars an hour by laboring Mexican people. These factories are

US owned and Mexico-based. Tarpaper shacks, the squatter-doms of the workers, and in town are banks for the wealthy and loan shops for the poor.

If internationalism was not working in favor of the rich and powerful, nationalism would continue.

"You have to crawl on your belly to get under fear. It's like a poison gas that floats at waist level. You can only subvert it by lying flat on your stomach and wiggling across the world like that."

When LA is north, you know you're really south. You drive north up the wall of the earth.

Don't ever turn your back to the water when you're in it.

In juvenile centers, the kids are all made to look alike, so no one will forget that they are as meaningless as numbers.

Okay, that's enough, said Tom. I know about juvenile centers. I am, after all, a lawyer. But you? How would you know anything like that?

Then she told him relentlessly about the place she had to stay while her children were in foster care. It was a halfway hell—a brick place where she was held in order to avoid a prison sentence for kidnapping her own children. While Tom listened, he gnawed at his cuticles and his knees jumped up and down nervously. Sometimes he even hummed so he wouldn't have to hear what she said, and he didn't hear, or if he did, he forgot.

Eight

I guess it was the next day we all crossed the border again on foot. She and the children with me. It was like leaving the end of the world and stepping into the beginning. I mean, for a few seconds, while you pass the beggars. Women with babies stuck to them. Clothes worn down like public carpeting. The faces were ancient as if cut from the turf. White people aren't so human, I think—so, in some sense—long-term. What do I mean by human? Imitations of Jesus? What do I mean by white? Individualists, loners. . . . Only inches, well, yards behind us, speeding freeways, pools behind motels, malls, gobs of food. It's all a cliché with nothing new to say.

We walked over a cement ramp stinking of piss and shit, past the first people in the world to the tourist strip where there were donkeys spray painted in zebra stripes, bars, taco stands, and lively full-faced humans. They were the citizens. The tourists had vacancy signs written in their flesh.

On sale: gold Rolexes, suede jogging shoes, leather vests, rainbow colored nylon hammocks, shiny urns, Disney ceramics, thick woven rugs and guaybera shirts. Everything seemed too expensive, even as a deal. As soon as an object has a lesser price than we would normally associate with it, it loses all its value. Then we start bartering greedily with the poor, asking them to lower their prices still further.

We went to a restaurant and talked, while Matty slept in a heap across her mother's knees, her wrists and ankles twitching and trembling as they sometimes did. Lee hoisted her little sister's feet onto her lap, and asked her mother what she did before she and Matty was born. I was a street person, Felicity said.

Yuck, said Lee.

Don't worry, it was okay, I learned a lot.

Did you love anyone then? I asked her. Who was nice to you?

She hid in her hair to reply.

I never met a kinder man than the homeless alcoholic who introduced me to the father of my kids. He was my teacher through a period of my life which was both an actual and an allegorical journey. He was very thin, ruddy, and ratty in his orange beard and brown clothes. His eyes were either squinting or seeking. Sometimes he turned into a handsome young man and men and women grabbed his hand in passing—as long as they wore gloves! He never liked me to see that and always released the woman's hand if I happened to glance back and catch him at it.

We had hope. That he would one day be free of his addiction and be able to love someone in health. Now I know we could never love each other more than we did then. Can you understand? Because this is important. We were wrecks, but our relationship was complete. Sufficient. Why ask for more? He was much worse off than I. But I was a lost spirit clad in a dirty pile of threads and we had to stumble through the rocky streets of the city to find our way out to the green woods where white dogwood bloomed in the spring before there was acid rain. We went along with each other, never having sex or even dreaming of it, and he told stories with such velocity and verve that I vowed I too one day would tell stories like that. The voice in the Garden of Eden just walked around without any flesh on; that was like us.

We were so physically needy that we were freed from our bodies and lived intense spirit-lives. We were the extreme forms that certain human emotions express, but repress too. Extreme affliction frees you, finally, from desire, and so we sought the longest and most difficult route to the nirvana of a woodland setting, hand in hand, mind you, and imagining a prospect both physical and internal. A white tree is reflected as a white tree in brown water. No matter what you want to say about it, I saw a pure soul when I saw him.

Lee didn't enjoy the story one bit, and asked if they could please go now—back to the hotel, or to look for a real place to live. Tom agreed with her—that they should leave and get serious about finding a home, and he carried Matty back through the hot streets to their car in a glittering lot. A mile of cars! He was feeling both claustrophobic and sad. Imagining his escape from this little afflicted clan made him suffer.

They went to the beach outside the hotel and swam as the day went. The salt water was a blessing, as sleep is, as breath and love are, and afterwards they lay on the sand, grateful for the wetness of the sea, Felicity hiding her face under a hotel towel while the girls dug in the brown sand.

I have to get this out of my system, she told Tom. I mean, what's been happening.

But why choose me to tell it to?

You're a lawyer. I keep telling you.

So? I don't know what that means.

You might be able to help.

I feel more like I'm receiving confession than seeing a client.

So go on. I'm listening.

Temple drove me to a ranch to pick up Matty. The place was an oasis—all green and deciduous in the humpty-dumpty hills. The air stank of cows and manure—I saw them grazing udder by tail in pens that extended for about a mile. They looked to me like containers of spirits in transit: midway between one life and the next, they patiently attended their passage by slaughter. And I didn't really believe in reincarnation the way I did in perdition.

Temple was dressed like a Wall Street broker. Smoked a joint which I refused to share, and babbled on and on about the evils of cigarette smoking, about the virtues of a vegetarian diet, about how the inherited rich were people who had done good in an earlier life. Money was their reward, he said. I said I didn't believe that God was really that involved with money and he shut me up by saying that it was money saving Matty's life, so I better believe something about money and power. I looked at him dumbfounded at the inconsistency of his thinking and remembered he was a sociopath and a mad man because of the way he was smiling.

And what, after all, was I? What was so consistent about me and my politics? All I was for that hour was a mother with one desire—to hold my child against me and hear her voice crying my name. I had been willing to do almost anything for that one event. The depths of my own murky ethics were never more known to me. My head throbbed and my throat dried and I thought of myself and Temple as two without faces. Once, when I was at the bottom of the pit as a drunk, I looked in the mirror and saw only glass and the image of the room behind me. There was no face there. I was gone. Now I felt the same horrifying absence of self-recognition. It would not go away and I leaned my head out the window for a breath of wind, as for the touch of the Lord.

Instead, the stink of cow meat was so strong, I had to pull my head in. Ahead I saw the house, and a veranda. Two men sat there, with Money and Matty between them. One got up and came to the car and backed out of the way while I ran to hug and examine Matty. She looked a little pale, thin, but well. Her smile was as wide as ever, and this time she didn't push me away but clung around me, no matter how I turned. Money told me she was fine, the physician said it would be a 12-hour operation, and take her a while to heal, but the chances of survival (for a few years anyway) were good as long as she took medication to prevent the organ being re-rejected. The medication would be very expensive, but Temple pushed me towards the car, saying he would take care of it. He slammed me and Matty in the back seat and proceeded to laugh and fool around with the two big guys outside.

Matty actually curled up around me and told me what had happened to her there. She called them all doctors, and she said they were nice, and did a lot of tests which didn't hurt. She said they X-rayed her insides after she drank something bitter, and that was the only bad part. She had watched endless videos and stayed in bed while Money hung around being nice.

Were they hopeful? I asked.

They said the operation would make me all better.

God, what bliss! I screamed and burst into tears.

Matty wiggled on my lap all the way back to the motel. She really only wanted to get to her sister, and so did I. But we had to act patient and submissive in the car. Temple was colder than usual. Flies settled on his cheeks. I was scared of setting him off on some cruel line of thought, and stayed quiet, squeezing Matty against me.

But even with the bad attitude coming off of Temple, for awhile I was really happy and filled with belief, and I rushed inside to tell Lee the good news as soon as we got back. Matty fell asleep. And Money sat outside with me in a patch of dull, desert-white sun, talking. She told me about Temple, about her own life, and about what she thought he wanted from me next.

When was this? Tom asked.

About a week ago.

And what did you learn?

"He says you have class," Money told Felicity. "He says some people are just born with it. It's the only kind of class he's interested in, he says, and you've got it. He wants you to work with him—"

But at what?

"—I've been doing some of it, but I'm no good because I don't have class? Ho! I don't even have sex for that matter. He was going to pay for me to have a sex change, you know, and that's how I got tied up with him. But I backed off at the last minute. I make more money the way I do it now than if I was an ordinary prostitute. It's true. They get a thrill, straight guys sneaking off with me. They're so scared they're gay, they can only do it with a guy in a dress. It's sad. Lucky for me. The macho ones, the marines, love it too, I tell you. So why would I get a sex change? Besides, I sort of believe in fate. This is me, for better or for worse."

Okay, said Felicity, I get the picture. But fill me in on the so-called operation Temple has going here. The one he wants me for.

"Available organs. He gets them on one side of the border and sends them to the other side. At least this is my impression."

What do you think he would do if I ran off, refused?

"Track you down, what else?"

Money lay back on the bed and yawned. She wore a gaudy green nylon dress and her silicone breasts oozed partway out of the straps close to her armpit. Under the silk was the bulge of her genitals beside a pouch of money, and under her stockings, black hair. She closed her eyes and Felicity was reminded—by her slack jaw, full lips, and sealed eyes—of an Incan statue made of rough gray stone staring through the leaves of a tropical forest. Felicity's throat thickened, she felt ill at the image of flesh becoming stone, and recognized it coming from a movie about the Amazon.

Nine

She climbed out from under her towel and got up abruptly off the sand. We were staring into the sunset, while the girls played on the shore outside the motel. She reminded me of the word CASBAH, with her pink glowing legs, back to the elements, an exhausted ocean, teeth chewing buckets of sand, the same doomed waters since Genesis, and a sky which was a theater for clouds and birds to perform in—swollen as if by a rainbow of emotions—and laying colors on every soft human face in sight. The children stood side by side while the foam tickled their ankle skin, squinting at the dolphins that sliced lines in the water. Creatures like black notes on water.

The girls were straight-limbed, their ribcages prominent, their thin arms long but muscular, their eyes large and luminous brown. I told Felicity I would stay with them while she returned to the motel. The dusk was gathering, reminding me that winter was not long past in the east. It wasn't late, and as the girls played with their hands in the languorous pink water, I turned off the ever-present mutter and grunt of traffic on the freeway and pretended we were off the coast of America, and somewhere safe. Safe from the life that Felicity was describing, and that was encroaching on every move we made. The coos and giggles of the girls seemed to stray in from an altogether different landscape. Matty backed up and sank into my lap, her bathing suit wet and cold on my legs. She twisted around and pulled open my mouth, looking inside.

Just looking for your real face! she explained, and jumped away and was gone back to the sea before I could grab her.

Next day, without much ado, we found them a bungalow abandoned by students, phone and t.v. included. It was a wreck on a highway between freeways. It faced a marsh where the water seemed to have torn the chaparral apart, which fed egrets and gulls, and the ocean fed it through channels under asphalt. Cars and trucks belted by her front door, sending up dust and water from blocked drains. This strip of highway was in a no-man's land, belonging neither to San Diego County nor to the next town over. Only a sheriff patrolled the road, and then hardly ever. Trains tore over the marsh; a long, long series of boxcars passed by at 3:15 A.M. Ants infested the house—tiny ones, no bigger than the dust that produced them; they were orderly, moving in strict formation, discovering a crumb on a shelf only minutes after it had fallen there. Their prescience suggested that there are ways of knowing the future and the past and the present all at once. Daddy long-legs and woodspiders played in every corner and wanted nothing so much as to survive. When the night came, the darkness was a substance as thick as water, and the stars were winks and jokes tickling its surface. The ocean thrashed around in the background, becoming thunderous when the cars subsided and the air was silent otherwise outside.

She had a spidery room with a sagging double bed and pink bureau, and the children had a double-decker bed on a glass porch in back. Tom slept on the couch, making elaborate plans out of dreams. They ate chicken, greens, and rice which she cooked with authority, throwing around garlic and onions and spices with her tiny efficient hands. A 12-inch television with poor reception could not dampen the joy of the children at having a place to call their own. During the day the military performed acrobatic aviation exercises in bat-shaped planes, riding out from the camp in the desert and over the sea where they disappeared mysteriously into the whiteness of far sky. Felicity and Tom were relaxing with each other, against his will. Their quarrels repeated history. He was revolted by her stories, which she insisted on telling, no matter what it did to him. And he began to become increasingly annoyed by her responses to people in authority.

Why didn't you pursue medical care for Matty here? he asked in the kitchen. It seems like you gave up awfully fast.

"The American Medical Association has made the country a slaughterhouse of the poor for years," she said, then spat on the ground just short of Tom's shoe and hurried into the living room talking over her shoulder. "Fuck you," she continued. "I did not give up fast. You weren't there. Without insurance and without any job or real living situation, they, the doctors, didn't get too interested in helping us. The one place that was nice said it would take ages to find her the right-size liver. This has been going on for two years. We've been in and out of every hospital with any kind of program in pediatric liver problems. It costs hundreds of thousands of dollars, no kidding, to get one. And even then it might not work. I don't trust doctors, it's true, but I went as far as I could with them. If I had been rich or powerful, it would have been a different story. The lucky get luckier. And how are they so lucky? At the cost of their fucking souls."

So okay, said Tom. Then what was wrong with Temple's deal? Why didn't you go through with it?

You really want to know? And who says I didn't?

It's not all over?

No. Give me some wine.

No.

Please?

No.

I remind you of your family?

Yes, right. You seem compelled to break even the laws you make for yourself. You subvert yourself!

All right, I won't say anymore, except this. Between the United States and Latin America, there's a trade going on in body parts. This is the free market, get it? I thought you were political. I thought you cared about what's going on. I'm telling you, it isn't fair!

Fair to who?

People like me, and Matty.

It never was fair to people like you.

Tom left the room and the house and stood on the edge of the highway with his hair closing over his ears each time a car passed. He felt contaminated, as if he had drunk insect repellent. The brown smog had settled on the rim of the sea and the air was dank and interior, like a vault rather than a greenhouse. The ocean was gray but its passionate salty smell was as pungent as ever and he inhaled the mist of it between jolts of exhaust. He felt the presence of his father in the air, but now as a mind and conscience, nothing physical. The conscience was instructing him to respond less bitterly and twistedly than he was. The conscience was telling him to be clear about what was happening. He tried. He surveyed the thicket of stories that lay in his memory behind him, the most recent unfelicitous stories. Temple worried him. He now believed Temple might even be behind his own presence there. He felt manipulated, and passive, and not without fear. These were his least favorite feelings, and produced a desire for revenge when he encountered them. To be a victim gave him no gratification; it did not prove to him that what he suspected about the world all along was at last being proved to him. No. To be a victim was hell for him.

On a warm May day when he was a boy of eight, Tom had to be taken to the hospital in an ambulance after a car hit him, while he was riding his bike. He lay bandaged and throbbing and passive and infantile in a ward at Children's Hospital for at least two weeks. His mother spent afternoons with him, his father evenings. He was wheeled around—his two broken legs raised before him and his broken arms splayed across his front—to witness children in worse condition than himself, though it was not always obvious. It was his mother who wanted to make sure he understood the meaning of luck.

On one of these trips, his mother, whistling, pushed him into a lounge and left him while she rushed off to buy some cigarettes. There was no one in the lounge, a television was playing soap operas, and outside the warm spring air had thickened into early summer. The limp and tender leaves of May—nearly yellow, weighted by spears of pollen—were already a darker green and he could just see the tip of a city tree looking robust, as if it were stretching with pleasure.

He waited for his mother impatiently and strained to see out the window to the world he longed to play in again. When she came back, though, she didn't pay any attention to his request to look outside, but wheeled him against a wall, sat down and began to talk to him about the years before his birth, to explain why she had never loved him and why he was now, obviously, the heir of her bad luck. He had seen children poke at wounded pigeons and insects to evoke a twitch from that small body with which they could feel not sympathy, but empathy. He had seen how they wanted that sense of extension and connection which the twitch of the little body confirmed. His mother's voice was the instrument which worked on him to make him twitch, as if to insist that only his response would confirm her sanity. He hardly breathed, though, as he listened to her ramble, and concealed all reaction in the white swaddling which held him. He felt as if he was all ears and little else, while the pains increased in his muscles and joints, over the hour that she spoke, until he was trying to commit suicide by holding his breath. Of course it didn't work, though his gasping gained him the high of a painkiller in the end. In that hour he acquired the desire for narcotics which returned to him later; he also acquired a dread of women who lamented, who whined, whose voices echoed with depression, who lost hope, who saw misery every way they turned. While he sat there, age eight, his mother told him that Pedro was a dangerous man. She said she didn't want Tom speaking to him at any time, or in any place. She said she was sure it was Pedro who had run him down with his car.

Why? Where is he? he had asked his mother in awhisper.

We don't know for sure. But this makes it clear that we have to make sure he never returns to Boston.

But I don't think it was him, Tom sighed.

The heave of her breath was all he needed to hear to know that what he thought was beneath her contempt. She had made up her mind; Pedro had tried to run him over. That breath, like a gust of autumn wind, blew away his confidence that it was not Pedro who drove the car. But even though he went silent, and he set aside—for years—all thought about that accident, and who might have driven the car—some bruise had malingered in his psyche, a sense of an injury that bound him to Pedro—a mutual injury.

Inside, Tom stood behind Felicity saying, "I'm leaving tomorrow to visit the prison and I don't know if I'll come back here."

Thanks a lot.

I'll come back under one condition. If you will go to the police and turn in Temple.

I can't. Matty. Remember?

I'm sure we can find someone else to do the transplant.

We can't. I've tried. I know.

It's hard for me to believe you've done all you can. Just knowing you this long makes me doubt you would know how to find help for her.

Then leave. I don't need you.

Okay, but you're making a fatal mistake over this.

Maybe I am. I have a problem with authority.

Not with Temple's authority you don't. There's no problem there.

He's not the kind of authority I mean.

I guess not. What kind do you mean?

I'm scared of men with guns. I really hate them. Of judges. Of law in general.

That's obvious. How soon do you have to see Temple again?

Obviously, it could be at any moment. Whenever Matty can be done—or whenever he needs me to work for him.

Then make up your mind. Grow up!

Oh come on, man. You're hassling me.

She slammed herself in the bathroom. Tom made sure the children were sleeping; it was night when he went out for a walk down the highway. It was pitch black, stars bristling or falling overhead, and coyotes shrieking from the canyons across the marsh. He believed he was in another country, the air was so sweet and clear, and he understood why every building here was like a temporary birdhouse and why lives were disposable as tissue. It had to do with the space and the sea, with the border and beyond. Here he could be a hobo in his own home, a tourist on his neighborhood street, a transient at work, and a derelict in his heart. His father was telling him—this something—was at his side talking and walking, bag in hand, and shoulders bent. "At night people are upside down," said the ghost, "By day upright. But in space there is no direction."

And this time Tom took notes from careful observation, to pass on to his brother Dan. "Daddy's ghost was shaped like a flagon," he wrote, "but it was the size of a cumulus cloud and the same consistency. Fluff from far off, a gray fog as I entered it. It rose up and up on any given edge, then vanished. Because of the appearance of this spirit, I can't help but think I've inherited Mum's insanity, and so please pray for the ghost to depart forever. I do, but I pray without faith, and so poor Daddy is stuck near earth with cloudloads of other ghosts whose children are equally faithless. The irony is this: if I were able to forgive him—which is what I think he wants me to do, in order to break loose from here—then I would have to forgive him, first, for failing to give me faith. And in order to forgive him for that failure, I would have to have faith!"

Back at the bungalow Felicity was lying in front of the television. Its image was a pile of wobbling iron bars, snow and blocks, but somewhere behind them was an erotic situation, running through a defective cable wire. Flashes of breast, nipple, buttocks and mouth cut through the snow and bars. The voices were adamant in their expression of excited contact.

What are you watching? he asked her. There's nothing there.

If you look carefully, you can see stuff.

Any more popsicles?

An orange and a grape.

Can I have the grape? he asked.

Why are you asking me?

I don't know.

When he returned to the living room with the popsicle, she announced she was going crazy from lust and only making it worse by watching nearly invisible figures on television. Then she turned it off while he picked up a book and pretended to read. Actually he was twirling the icy popsicle between his lips and over his tongue and peering at Felicity who was herself nearly invisible under a blanket.

Are you happy? he called out.

For this house, yes, thank you.

No, I mean are you happy in yourself, now?

No.

I didn't think so.

Are you?

No, I want to move on and finish what I came here for. You have introduced me to a level of corruption that I never wanted to encounter. Now that I have, I can't really relax.

So what would make you relax?

Reporting it to the police. If it's true.

He'll kill me. Literally, she said.

Chances are, he will anyway. If it's true.

Thanks, guy.

I just want you to face the realities.

I have. You're going to leave us here alone.

You were alone before.

True. So go.

I'm going to call my brother.

It's awfully late in New York.

He never sleeps much.

I hope he's nicer than you.

It's just that he escaped. Home. Mother.

She twisted herself up in the battered armchair, with the blanket bent around her shoulders, and listened to his conversation with his brother. Tom told Dan everything—her whole story, where he was, and why, and what the phone number was; he told him Temple's name and asked what he should do. Then he listened for a long time, his expression registering change as fast as a television screen. His dark waves of hair looped around his ears, he kept twirling them in one finger. His face was gloomy with the shadow of a beard, his lips purple from the popsicle juice. He concluded his conversation with Dan by telling him he would be seeing his father, Pedro, the next day. It was evident to Felicity that Dan hung up in his face in response.

Tom put the phone down gently and she leaned over and said, "Let me look at your teeth," and she went over and pulled up his lip. You had braces, didn't you, I can see the line of a band with a purple stain. They're really white and straight. Why do you tell your brother everything? You act like he's your conscience or your twin.

He's my best friend.

Gimme a bite, she said and snapped off the tip of the purple ice, smiling down at him.

He leaned away, and back, and looked at her feet. My brother says I should leave you. And never come back.

That's really thoughtful, she said and sat down on his knees, facing him. Have you got a hairy chest like your legs?

Tom made no move, but sat still as if afraid she would fall. He addressed her neck when he spoke.

Leave me alone, Felicity, get up. I don't like you that way.

What way?

Intimate.

Why not?

You just aren't my type.

Can't we just fool around?

No, not when my mind is full of images of sick children and surgeons and Temple getting away with it. Sorry, but my mind effects my body.

How would sex interfere with that relationship?

It's just impossible.

She pressed her chest against him, her arms across his shoulders, her cheek against his.

Just so we know it's all still working.

What all? The parts of the machine. Body parts?

Come on, don't be so grumpy.

Uh uh. Get off.

Do I have to? I know you're leaving. I just feel lonely, scared, and why not. You're the sexiest man in the room.

You think Temple knows I'm here, right?

Obviously. He's coming to get me, don't you understand? Why do you think I'm scared? I don't want to do what he wants me to do, but because of Matty, I may have to.

I'm sure you will do whatever he wants. You always have.

She pulled up and jumped off of him. And now he followed her into her bedroom and watched her slip into the closet to undress and change into a pair of boy's pajamas. She was ignoring him, or pretending to.

The effect of her indifference was powerful, now, far more powerful than her interest. Mesmerized by her distance, he felt the loops of pleasure binding him to the flesh between his navel and his crotch. Like most boys he became sexually aware, through his own manipulations, in early adolescence. For him, though, this activity was sufficient for his survival, and in fact it filled him with confidence to know that he could always go off alone and seek a rush from his vigorous imaginings. He needed no one's help. However, the long-term effect—because this activity did continue for years, even when he was in bed beside a woman—was to separate him from the world to the point where the material order of things was more of a representation than a reality. He observed life as others look in store windows, or up at movie screens. And when he looked in the mirror at himself, he was always greeted by the image of a stranger—someone much thinner, darker, more intense than he felt himself to be.

A woman for him was also a representation in his imagination, not an actual being, and in order to complete their collaboration, he had to become a representative of himself—a mutual invention, a double of the one doing the imagining. He had special places to which "I" would travel with the shadowy figure of a woman—to ramshackle mobile homes on the edge of a forest. And there he would suffer and enjoy at her mercy, a mercy which was experienced through his own hands, not "hers." She waited for "me."

In the world he moved around like one slightly dazzled, or defeated, unable to participate fully in any social gathering, because of his eagerness to get home to his appointment with "I" and "she" in his closet. Door shut. Yet the process, like all processes, was subject to entropy, and he had recently lost heart for it.

Only now when Felicity emerged from her closet in a torrent of hair did he feel his loneliness had a location on his body, and he recognized her as a candidate for his imagination, she being a pariah—a social enemy—an extra at the table of the world. The forgotten one. The place not set. The empty chair. The undesirable who only "I" discovered, and whose indifference made no difference.

At the threshold of her room he announced his resentment of her lack of interest in him. "You never show any interest in me," he said. "That is, in my trip to visit my brother's father. It's always you, and your problems."

She protested, requested more information about his plans, but suddenly he was not an articulate man. His throat stuck, his mouth was no avenue for his thoughts, no chute down.

He said "Oh never mind," and goodnight, and went to lie in the other room's darkness, where he could conjure up the familiar one, and not Felicity, to comfort him. At first, and this was unusual, he imagined a tunnel of semen sending up shouts, songs, laughter, whispers, cries—of unborn thousands—violinists, graphic designers, greenhouse builders, divorce professionals, pet groomers, clergy people, bus drivers, accountants, diamond importers, civil servants, sand blasters, models, cleaners, truckers, mountain climbers, athletes, addicts, divas, poets, politicians, saints, lovers—all those children trapped in his own groin.

And then he found his way to the forest. And the arc of his two closed eyes formed twin smiles.

She came in a season of thick fog—Indian summer—emerging like a peacock through falling cards. General outward moisture now brightened his aura of luminous gold. The gold of a loaf of bread held in the lap of a poor man.

For the time being there were people to be discarded. She was a protection by helping him deal with the tiresome ones. He could only take things as they came. When, later, he accepted her judgements, she was hurt by his corrections.

He didn't need one more advisor, and was always surrounded. He directed this confusion like a captain, as out of a capsized boat, there's a rush.

Then into an excavation, not like Pompeii, but in the way the autumn day looked. Like a pack of cards. Large faces and colors. And she was sympathetic, not sarcastic, this time. The windup of their communion—a walk—put them as if in a boat together, pushed up and down a current.

After some trauma, he always took their trust for granted. The crouching kitten will, in time, kill the little gray bird. He wondered what she wanted.

She got inside his idea of himself, he didn't know when. She knew how good he looked, but this didn't help him adore her. Just

her possession (entrance) into how he felt—always about himself—and he sensed her measuring and weighing his deeds as he'd
do to himself, but more.

She was the spot concealed in his folds. The secret of her own
life formed her protective entrance into his idea of himself. He fell
short, but looked bigger. Better. He tossed their intimacy with in-
timations of defeat. Don't get the wrong idea. Passing cars assured his ears that sound was motion.

There are days when we have thought almost everything there
is to think.

"I am, you say, a man of vision?" he asked her.

The end of your watching will lead to a view.

Recalls and results ran circles around them. She helped him to
pass for a man like any other, but he was a bird of clipped, drawn
wings. Into this egoistic gather, he relapsed, handsomely. Had another of his waits, while she watched.

Vertiginous orange air, a plummet and a yardstick on the void.
The chill of a shock. Fog's catastrophic old fashioned fare.

She was almost old always. And medium-sorry for him. Scarce
a corner of their October was orderly. Like Fall in a valley of
bankrupt branches, her poverty was BETTER than his failures.

No thought is sufficient to the day's bread, she knew about. An
unlooked-for twist in the cavernous hours has possible rewards,
was his style report.

She was washed by fog as if she was drawn in soft silver sand.
She threatened the presence of trees by one desire—not to be seen.
A sadness effective as a week of cool intervals. Visions as little as
flame tips.

His was a cold light on something rained and orange, though
she whom he couldn't escape was part of the effect. Like the erotic
hidings under some objective purpose, or a cat stayed kittenish, she
was a delicate gray, serene as a dove.

The high flicker of her intelligent fires made the furniture of nature brighter. It was no costume weather, after all, not theater. Walking with longing made consummation fall behind.

She'd shown him nothing but more rickety shacks he should know about, and an outer stiffness making things fall. A pencil on the path. A joy too much for consciousness to bear makes a bad balance, an imperfect contract.

He and she had many more years of staying apart before they could really hurt each other.

Draped, soft, forlorn in her slimness. She was the wisecracking kind who clutches herself as stiff as the word I.

Two morsels of bread and bread, their appetites were still not nearly satisfied. Her hand kept him waiting. She turned the lights on in.

Sprinklers twirled adjoining mists. She had something more to give him: the nothing that was something.

Even before you know a fact, it's true. In the most besotted impression, there's coming information.

His gasp filled the air with more mood. Instilled as a hope and stroke in the limited atmosphere. Small chance. Even as, perhaps because, connection didn't come, his consequent passion was to possess. He would lose her for this, though there's no being sure.

She took up the hose and water met. Rainbow's the spouse of fog. Eyes continued to be attached to her his, and occasional egoistic latching, as if he looked for a key to a clock so he'd be in control of the time that they touched.

She prays her stars will be invisible. Dipper and sprinkler, the fragrance moisture elicits and can't be seen. Treading the earth, around and around, gravely. The OTHER side was what they didn't, couldn't, know. Mystification waded through the unbeaten paths.

The way truth welcomes, then rejects you. The way recognition of the really good feels like a blinding.

An anomaly of lack, abstention like abstraction—all NOT. She repeated and repeated, in fact to surprise him. He was.

Constancy shocks. But abrupt cessations did what they could in this case. Speculations love company. So she was grieving at his departure as soon as he was there. Graven tablets sprang out of the garden she tended. All engraved with their names in some captive cupidity.

Like a disconsolate, she roamed around with callouses, pencils and work to do.

The turn of her chin was superficially slight towards him, as to mean insufferable joy. He was, for that time, a maestro.

If the body is bread, his was a loaf she'd never eat, and she began to accept, too, the loss of silver, good luck, fame, in his and her days. So his postponement of possessing her was part of their scheme. It was to lead her where we allow the benefit of a doubt.

A smoking torch nonetheless still gathered her skills for human touch together inside her. He'd never want to know that. Her plans were always surprised by her approach into them. So she stayed hidden.

His intentions, meanwhile, were being met elsewhere, full of face and handling. He was addicted to orgasm. She had something else to give him which he didn't even consider. While he stoked the leaf tops mentally as if his thought was a responsible form.

She knew she'd pass from mood to move, as an exercise in giving up. Painting the sets. A door wasn't shut in any position of the steamy air. Buttery, light-colored leaves. And he could live a worthy life if she just knew how to tell him, so he'd understand, but she didn't.

He couldn't control or alter his inclinations, and his character was such that his sharp edges were gilding.

She didn't invent him, or the words he held on his lips. It only confirmed the authority he conferred on her that her presence made this particular wording possible. "I will do what is necessary to keep you safe."

A small branch snapped and fell into her hair.

The walk was a circle, shaped like a house, all edge and abutment, with whirling only in colors and gray. They kept two full bodies of air between them, not loafing, not rushing.

Having made his statement he washed his hands of all her questions, his curiosity was perfunctory. Now here, she did make another pause, which surprised him, as if she had abandoned her presence inside.

But he inhaled, and she was taken in, restored to his imagination, amusing as all expectations without.

He reached his door then and her anguish crossed the threshold. "Don't do anything to hurt me," she said. He winced as if the three or four things he most wanted to do would have to be put off, if they would ever by done at all. And much pain did it cause them, much, to step apart. He had a dreadful sense of standing before her for the last time.

A flight of chats. Let others be responsible for his guilt. He would attend to her needs, in spite of the consequences, and ask nothing in return. She sensed his concession and fell on her knees before him. "I," she whispered, "am he whom you know." He leaned to meet her, mouth and hands upraised. She was no shadow.

Ten

The next morning Tom left to drive east, before anyone else was awake in the house. The terrain was flat, brown, baked. The social aura was venomous, redneck. He sensed it. He wrote on a large legal pad on the car seat beside him. His mind was alert and overcharged with language. He wrote to get rid of words. He tried to place Pedro in his past, and then to resurrect him from that ashy zone. Flying elements of thought and memory shot between his ears. His hand was tense on the pen, and shaking.

"The body is the first mask; what it does is only partial evidence of what is concealed inside. When the body is gone and the spirit is left naked and transparent, the essence of personality exists with a potency undreamed-of. It is easier to feel the presence of a bodiless spirit than any person you might sit and talk with—that is, if love is involved. I personally am much better at loving from a distance."

"To paraphrase an experience is a heresy, unless you can turn the paraphrase into an organic part of that experience. This is what confession does. This is what I will try to do, keeping in mind the terrors of earlier heresies, like Docetism, Marcionism, Adoptionism, Sabellianism, Nestorianism, Gnosticism, Pelagianism, Arianism. . . . If you paraphrase correctly, you must reproduce the original in its emotional and moral content. I mean, this is what I believe. I must reproduce the feeling of the original moments!"

145

REMEMBER, exiled in myself

Sorry to disappoint
you but I am
a poet.

the hell globe of info

if you don't KNOW
where you are, you are
of nature + soul, Lost, you are

KNOW
No...

Jesus ONLY appears where there are
Lips of bodies.

Diva - bird, of God
Dante's embankment is
NUMBER. Routine —
that is, suffering.

— What is it TO KNOW

Earthly Spirit
is for
the lonely
spirits

Health / education

I don't
know
people.

KNOW = HOME

Let's secede from the smug

POVERTY NO HOPE — HEART/CHILDREN

"A ghost is the opposite of an angel. A ghost carries the residue—or after-image—of its earthly existence. It's like a leaden emotion, laden with recollection. An angel has never experienced the earth as a sensual event, even though it may aspire to; a ghost yearns away from the object the angel envies. A ghost however still has a few last things to say. (What is the difference between the spirit and the soul, it might ask. The soul belongs to you personally, it might answer, and it is the accountant of your deeds. The spirit on the other hand is nothing personal. You live IN the spirit)."

The experience of throwing something ahead of me, as a child, and then running after it, was like the experience of aspiration and accomplishment in later years. The memory of my brother skipping stones across the top of the gray sea is like a painting of that experience. Utopian. I see his soft brown face squinting at a sulphurous sun and a smile wide on his lips as he jerks his elbows and the flat rock hops over the top again and again. That skipping action dazzled him and me, watching from a boulder. I never tried to do what he did well. . . I remember feeling the potential for heroism in Pedro's person, even way back, when he took Dan and me for walks in parks, especially the Arboretum. And the zoo. I remember he was tall, dark-skinned and fast-walking, with spectacles and a pair of enormous hands. He pulled us along, quickly, breathing hard from smoke and rattling off the names of the surrounding flowers and animals. Just as the shadow from a statue makes it seem alive, so the shadow from Pedro reminded me that he was not just bigger, but deeper, than me. In his presence I usually experienced a sense of largeness and power. It must have been the presence of the Hell from which he came and to which he was going.

The prison was on the desert, only a few miles from the border. On the way the language of the landscape was new to Tom: *chaparral, sage, mesa, arroyo, mesquite.* Hot as an oven, and as dry, the air might explode if he lit a match. If he hadn't had air conditioning he would've swooned in the car seat and crashed. His nerves were already boiling. Thirty-three years: this was the end of only imagining Pedro. He felt it strongly: each day is the end of a story, each day is an anniversary, but some have more magnitude than others. He had an erection and had to wait in the car till his thoughts could drive it down and away. How to deal with the coming hour, when he would finally see Pedro, again, he didn't know. He had to trust that the soul of the man would be unaltered and familiar to him; that it would not have changed in density or dimension or quality. "Technology is like an extra and artificial limb attached to the natural world," he mused. "How could the varied planet be viewed as insufficient? Why do we keep needing to add more? This drive to that building—has been almost Biblical—how could my parents have let this man rot in here and never reached out to him once?"

Tom parked in front of the yellow penitentiary where people who had committed crimes against society were cordoned off and guarded night and day. The building cast a long shadow.

Inside, there was a lounge and a booth where he checked in. He was frisked, thoroughly, stripped of extra articles, and sent through four heavy doors before he was told to sit down in another lounge area, this one containing several red vinyl seats with what looked like bite marks on them. A sad woman sat at one end of the room and he placed himself away from her and waited until he was led by a guard into a very small room. Foam rubber popped through the cracks in two green chairs; an ashtray wobbled on a steel stand. The walls were pea green, like the clothes on the guard.

Pedro was admitted almost immediately. He was a tall bent-over man in his late sixties, white haired, with a soft brown complexion. His eyes were long and papery, his lips thick and dry, and his teeth rotten. He had deep grooves in his cheeks which thickened when he greeted Tom. His eyes gleamed like garnet. He wore brown.

They sat across from each other and Pedro immediately lit a Camel, which he smoked with the intensity of someone chewing chocolate. His voice was gravelly when he asked Tom why he had come after so many years. When Tom began to respond, he stopped him, asking, And how's your father?

He passed away—recently.

And your mother?

Mum? She's still alive.

In the same place?

Yes.

And Danny?

   He lives in New York.

Married?

   No. He works like Daddy—as a printer—for a printer.

You're thinner than I imagined you. What?

   Yes, I'm sure, said Tom.

Why did you come here anyway?

   I just want to know about you, do you mind? How much more time do you have to spend here?

My time will be up in five years, then I won't know where to go or how to live.

   I'm sure you'll surprise yourself.

No chance of that. All the surprises have come from elsewhere. Not from myself. Your father was my best friend. Did you know that? What? He took me in, took care of me. Your mother was already my partner, though it was never legalized. Like all women she turned out to be deceiving and a whore.

   I'm not so—

What? Women. They're much more complex than men. They have these bottomless desires. They want and want and want, and the more you give them, the more they want. Better to hold it all back from day one and let them learn discipline. Every story from every man in here repeats that statement. Women are driven by their bodies, their desires, your mother was no exception, not even with her mental problems which came from her intelligence. She was very smart, as you must know, but a victim of a deranged appetite—for the new, the unknown. When she couldn't satisfy her craving for the delicious new experience, she drank her way into oblivion.

I know about my mother.

What? You were fat as a boy. You had the personality of a fat boy too. Loud and needy. She must have destroyed you, too. I only recognize your eyes. What happened? I can guess what happened. And your father, did she ruin him too?

Probably.

Of course she did, not probably. He was easy prey. Decent but cowardly. He was the type who did more damage by his decency than he ever could have done by being a son of a bitch. Not that smart, but committed, which makes up for a lot. He let himself be used, picked apart by the people around him, so-called Fellow Travelers. His painting was only mediocre. That was the real tragedy of his life. He was second-rate, and he worked his ass off at it anyway, as if he didn't know it. He knew it. She knew it. There is nothing more unnecessary to the world than a bad artist.

I think she likes his work. Liked.

What? If he had put those energies of his into some worth-while human work, his life would have been justified, but instead he scraped by with derivative oils on canvas.

I really just wanted to know about you.

What's to know? The story ended a long time ago. Since then it's just been thought. No story, no action. What? Your parents had me locked up. They threw away the key. And they went on with their own lives.

But after you left Boston—

What? Boston? I didn't leave voluntarily. I was driven out of Boston. They put out a warrant. Saying I tried to kill you. Why would I kill a little boy? For what? I had to go underground, change my identity. But they knew where I was. We belonged to the same party. We had the same contacts.

You really believe they put out a warrant?

I don't believe it, I know it. What? Your mother could always get her way, no matter what it took. She did it by erasing the connections between things. So she'd never feel responsible.

I guess you never remarried.

What? I never married in the first place. But I got another gal pregnant before I made the mistake of shooting a man. You want to hear what happened? I was undertaking to raise funds for those witnesses who had been summoned before HUAC, I was assaulted from behind, and somebody shot him. Guess who got tagged for the crime? Correct. What? When I wrote for help to your father, he never even answered. So here I was put, and here I remain. . . . So what's your life story?

I practice law—it's a small legal-aid firm, we have an office on Tremont Street, remember that, in Roxbury? Mission Hill, across from the cathedral, basilica—

Run by the recidivists, or whatever that order is called.

Redemptorist. One of them is a healing priest. Mother goes there. To him.

She needs it. You can tell her from me that she comes up in my dreams, as a fiend, a devil-figure, even now, so many years later. Why did you come see me instead of Dan? After all, he's my son, not you, you came from the loins of the harpy and the traitor.

He didn't want to.

Well, tell him he's making a mistake. Could be fatal. I've got emphysema.

Does anyone—from outside—?

Three women keep in touch with me. It's always women who have guts in the end. It's always women who act from the heart. It's women who cross boundaries. Not men. A lady lawyer, a hooker from Winnemucca, Nevada, and Dan's half sister, a gal you certainly don't know. They keep me going.

Where's the half sister?

Her name is Billie. She lives across the border, works at a hotel outside Ensenada, she's clean, about twenty-six.

What hotel?

You really want to know? The Mira Vista.

Billie what?

My name of course. You might like her. You and Dan. Have a family reunion down there on the beach. What? I remember you liked the water. The tub. Your mother didn't much like you, that's why she stuffed you with food. Every time you fell or got hurt, she'd pack you with cookies and go on directing her attention elsewhere. She was ashamed of what she did to me. She was ashamed of Dan's African features. She compensated by dumping on you. And the joke is, you were darker than Danny, your skin color, still is, I bet, Ha! Danny was high yellow, you're brown, like your father. She was the type of white woman who hooks into a black man to be validated politically, but really she despises him. I remember how shitty she treated you, just because of your brown skin, and there was lots of it! She probably turned Danny gay. What about it?

No.

Your father loved you though. I guess you know that.

He also loved my brother, said Tom.

What? He stole Danny away from me. He better have loved him. Whatever that means. Action is all it means. You think the world is full of talk and no action? You know what it's really full of? Silence. . . . Well, go on now and build your own prison, boy, before others build one for you—one that doesn't fit any crime you know of.

Tom stood up obediently as Pedro began a fit of coughing. He went to the door and turned his back on the old man while he brushed his burning eyes. He knocked and almost at once the guard opened up to let him out. He didn't say good-bye or look back to wave to Pedro.

In his car, he drove without seeing, then got lost, totally insensible to the roads he was taking. This way he ended up beside the hills along the border, where rangers shoot smugglers who shoot and rob Mexicans who are illegally entering the country. There was litter everywhere down along the fence—parts of engines, car seats, styrofoam and the underwear off escaping people. High tall grass like bamboo shoots was strung with boxers and shirts and socks, and dust blew up from under the tires of raging American vans off to the west of him.

He recalled an image from a movie where the men throw an object in a white cloth ahead of them as they move through the gloaming towards an unknown goal. The object flies and falls, proving they can, also, pass through that zone. That was an image of the way human lives are lived—thoughts, plans, calendars thrown ahead into the void; he understood it. But something about time was skewed and he felt like one who has come to the end of his energies.

Other remarks, made by Pedro, returned to him now:

"You know what I learned, after all that shit and this miserable life? It'll surprise you. Any enterprise worth its salt is directed toward the relief of human suffering. This includes technology, science, art, politics, music, etcetera. What? Surprise you? Even a plain book—or painting—if it's any good, and your father's painting was not—makes suffering clear so the human reader can be relieved of pain. As far as I can tell we are here to seek cures to our rotten condition. I wonder why the whole world isn't as psychotic as your mother. It might as well be, it probably is. What? The United States Government is medieval if it isn't psychotic. The terms are laid down by science and technology, by systems of measurement. I'm writing a book about money. Marx is the only one in the last hundred years who has really taken it on as a subject, and now it's time for a new one. Science is the new narrative of our civilization, so soon it will absorb the old monetary values and we will begin to measure reality and social principles solely in terms of computer technology. Wait and see. You already see a praying mantis on TV dancing to Bach. You see brains being dissected to a background of Miles Davis. The circuits are crossed. A trap made of numbers. What? The world is a museum. We have been colonized by our own government. The point is, with all this talk these days about culture, each person wants nothing more than to be liberated from the accoutrements of so-called culture. And what is culture? Kitsch. Who did I kill and why? No one. What? I was jumped by an informer at a meeting many years ago. And now I'm in for murder. The real killer went free, I was framed, but no one cares, even if they believe me. Science wins."

The words seemed to loop across the roof of the car, and to slide down the windshield, and Tom drove recklessly back the way he had come (a motion which contradicted his sense of termination). He let the wind whip at his arm and face and upper frame. Wind was the closest thing to water he could get for that hour. Water was what he was really after. Water to wash off every last residue of his time with Pedro. He felt he literally had time on his hands. A slick smear of it dotted with grime. Time, grime. Slick, illicit.

He had visited prisoners before. Prison always sickened him, but never so violently as this one. This time. The paradox of a place lost to the world being the very place most locked and sealed upon the face of the world—and in it Pedro—forgotten by the couple who were known to be activists—committed to the poor and displaced—his mother, his father. How did every citizen end up collaborating in the technique of silence?

"Maybe Pedro was lying. It's so hard to believe. . . ."

Tom scanned the sky and the distant mountains thinking how good they were to the human eye. Why, he wondered, even in the thick of despair, does a person yearn, with a whole heart, for something good, something complete? Why, even on this brown sandpile, did his heart swing up to the places most linked to childhood—the snow on the windowpanes, or soft summer rain in the trees—to a face filled with the love bestowed on it by the very person dreaming of that face, his brother in this case? Why did he, stuck in the indulgence of time, and sad, still find himself driven forward automatically (platonically) towards the beautiful?

Am I responsible for creating tomorrow's objects and events out of my motions, or is it already waiting for me—a table set, a pair of hands producing food?

All he could really remember was the statement Pedro made about women. Not his mother, but others. And he wanted to see Felicity now. To tell Matty that the human spirit is the size of a bird, and that's why the holy spirit is always represented as a bird. To tell his brother that Pedro had the integrity of the stereotype and he should at least visit him. To tell Lee that she must learn to enjoy herself before it's too late. To tell the ghost of his father that he had in his life failed to live up to his words about brotherhood. To call his mother and tell her he would be staying longer than he planned.

When he got to the little house, Felicity and the girls were not there. No note told where they had gone, but there were tire marks in the doe-colored sand outside the house, not his own. He paced around, eating tortillas and cheese with his hands, and drinking Coke. He looked closely at the undeveloped land, so to speak, around the house. Jasmine, dichondra, poppies in the dust. Pepper trees tilted over a chainlink fence and a bamboo jungle struggled to break into the lot. In the background, where ravines were purple with ice plant, someone had hung a wind chime made of varnished seashells in the pepper trees. Shingles, tiles, tar and rusty hubcaps were tossed in a ditch. The walls inside the house were made of cork.

Roaming the empty house, he found odds and ends scattered as if they all left in a hurry. The clothes of the children moved him. He touched and folded little pairs of shorts and shirts and put them away. As he did, confused, he imagined saving Felicity and the children from Temple. But then he didn't dare interfere, because for the first time in many years he felt himself to be outside the law. Careless. Dislocated. He began to pack up everything he owned, and to stow it in his car. He decided he was at liberty to do whatever he wanted, and at once he began to know what he wanted as he disposed of his attachment to Felicity and the children. They, he decided, already had someone watching over them. No matter how vile Temple was, he was the master Felicity had chosen. And he had, after all, done his duty by finding them a place to live. No one had asked more from him than that, a fact for which he thanked God, as he took a long shower in lukewarm water.

Eleven

And so, now clean again, Tom left and drove south through San Ysidro and National City, to the border and over. He drove through the abrasive hills, coastally, from Tijuana south to Ensenada and south some more. The great swells of mountain bracken and cliffs to the sea were lathered with the shampoo yellow light he had come to associate with the word California.

In a beach community he found the Mira Vista Hotel. There he rented a room for two nights and sat on the terrace to drink a Coke and sop up salsa with chips. His eyes were weeping though tears did not emerge. The lashes were damp. The sea glittered like Christmas as he imagined the girl, Billie, to be each one of the waitresses. Stocky, dark, serene, smiling? One cute one wore a cap to hold up all her hair and had American manners and attitudes. She was busy behind a small outdoor bar. The time was mid-afternoon. Citrus trees and roses were planted around. Crochet baskets hung full of geranium. The sun had an intense journey here—much more like an airplane on a trip under four hundred miles than a long distance ride. Up and down. But perplexedly, it stayed light longer, later, earlier. Old water where the fishing boats trailed beyond the laugh of the breakers.

Which one was Billie? He finally asked. The cute waitress answered that Billie wouldn't be in to work till five; then she would be there all night. Tom gave a message, his room number, and walked between horses along the seashore, shoes in hand, and plotted and planned: if he was in charge of a country, would it be like this one and how. A place to disappear in, as Felicity had done. But he didn't linger over thoughts of her, he thought of a future which did not include her instead, and then went into a rickety seaside restaurant and called his brother in New York where it was night, the day over, events completed, people trying to forget this and that. He ordered Dan to join him and heard both temptation and hesitation on the line. Come on, come on, he whined and told his brother where to find him and how. Then he sat at a shaky table facing the sunset and drank juice. Lost colors sought form in the sky. An astronaut said that in outer space there are more colors than we have here.

In the night he dreamed he met Billie and between them there was a bond, instantaneous and pathetic. She turned when he came onto the terrace and saw he was the one she had always been waiting for. He was less aroused, or certain, until he was close up, beside her, and telling her his name and why he was there. Then he looked at her like a possession, because that was the way he felt, and he let her seat him, then sat beside him, while he blurted out specific hidden facts about himself: I was drug-addicted for a couple of years, I have never been able to love anyone wholeheartedly, I'm dying of loneliness. . . . All this was said quickly, and nearly at once. The experience was more primitive than romantic. There was no air between them that did not contain the spirit of the other. She didn't move much, except in lots of little ways, nervous motions of hands and eyelids and lips and shoulders, while she sat erect and perfected on the edge of her seat. She was breathing him in like a little animal composed of fear that twitches and sniffs each time it pauses.

She was smooth as honey, and its same color, with soft features, a full sloping mouth, and the garnet eyes of both Pedro and Dan. She was unadorned, unmade-up, dressed in a white middy blouse and blue uniform skirt, for her job. Her black hair was looped into a braid and a bun. At one angle she was sixteen, at another forty, no in-between. There were three ways she resembled Dan: her eyes, her lips and her delicate long hands. She was, even with all the above, not a striking beauty but a hidden one. He was sure she could pass through (had) all her days unnoticed, unloved, like a reddish stone under a stream. But now that he had found her, everyone would take notice of her—a fact he sat and regretted, one which made him hesitate, but not seriously, before moving forward.

While she worked he lay on his bed and listened to the radio. Most of the stations played Mexican pop, except for one where he heard Motown. It reminded him of his little office, his clients in that cold mean climate, the troubling disorder of black urban life, he felt his blood race. The frontier was a fortress. Every dog loves a daddy. His whole body was suffering there like the artwork described by Pedro. His hands were clasped and aching under his head, his bare feet clawed at each other, he listened and waited for her to knock on his door.

When she did she looked almost exactly like the woman in the dream. He proceeded to blurt out specific hidden facts about himself, to tell her why he was there. Just to see. A family member. I think I'm a primitive. I need a tribe. Help me, I'm dying of loneliness. They talked until the sky whitened into the film of a new day and then she, promiscuous and incapable of commitment, joined him under his blankets and they played with each other's bodies. This went on all the day into the afternoon, she was an expert at anything involving her hands, and then he got a call from the desk that his brother was on his way down from San Diego. Tom sang with a chest drawn tight as a drum as she showered, his throat knotted and cracked. He washed her long hair. She, behind his back, stuck her fingers in around his tongue, massaging his gums, and resting her own mouth against his ear, called him her brother.

Fog rolled in overnight from the sea. It moved around the canyons, swallowing greens and browns and turning the earth as white as the sky. It was restless, as if an army of ghosts were seeking out guerrilla activity on the lowest coast of California. This fog stretched way down into Baja drawing with it a smell of deep seas. Whiteness and more whiteness. Helicopters rested. The airport shut down. It was a field day for human coyotes sneaking people over the border. That same army of ghosts was for this day protecting illegal entry into America. Dan had been rerouted to Los Angeles and drove a rented car south from there; it took about five hours to get to Ensenada, where the whiteness screened and softened his first views of Mexico.

He found his brother with a woman on his knees. Her name was Billie, she looked familiar, so the fact that she was his half sister seemed to work on the surface of things. He watched them from the entrance to the terrace at the motel. The fog had made Tom's kinky curls go haywire. The woman was dealing with this, tying his hair into a tail with a thick elastic, her elbows on his shoulders. Dan called Tom.

The woman jumped off his lap as Tom leaped to his feet and rushed to greet his brother with an embrace. Dan's reaction was to recoil. He was not an enthusiastic man, but sensitive and uncertain. He was very thin and moved as if he couldn't see. His skin was caramel, his mouth red and wide, his hair nappy, and he gave the immediate impression of being repelled. Tom clumsily handed him a chair and danced around him, worshipping and worrying. Dan wore a lopsided smile; he always smiled on one half of his face only. But he accepted the offer of a Coke and a plate of food. He asked no questions but appraised his brother and the half sister. Her complexion was sallow, her features conventionally pretty, her eyes round and brown. Her arms were straight, thin, streaked with dark hair, and her hands were small and unusually shapely. The hands alone were similar to his own, and he took one of them and then held them together, appraising the likeness of bone structure, color of the palm and its shape, back to the wrist where it changed and each was alien to the other. He chalked up the familiarity of her face to its conventionality and watched her watch Tom.

They were moist, enclosed by the wall of fog, the only ones out on the terrace. It seemed like a snow, and was exciting as snow can be. They remembered mornings of snow they awoke to in the South End of Boston, pigeons cooing in the eaves, the way the white stuck to the brick and melted for the traffic outside. But they were here encircled by wild geranium, fuchsia, ficus, and pepper and palm trees. They sat at the round table and spoke to each other in soft voices. She told Dan her story, as she had told it to Tom already, and Dan told them what he had been doing, and Tom didn't mention Felicity or the girls but only his days looking at San

Diego. "It's really still part Mexico as far as Oceanside where the last border patrol is. You're not really back in America until you're about an hour north of the border."

Billie did not like her father and told Dan that. The way she didn't like him was firm, like a decision she had made for which she felt proud. But then she said she would never abandon him. She was sunny, a warm soul, as they say, with complexities postponed or swallowed. She lived in the moment, moaning with pleasure over every bite of food and sip of wine, swearing she feared nothing and no one, had no regrets, rarely thought of the future, and she spoke of her lust for Tom openly, and only obliquely referred to the time she spent blissed out, in ecstasy, numb, crystallized, stoned. For that experience she spent some time in prison where she was rehabilitated. Dan meantime loved his wine. As the fog blued and blurred with the setting sun, they ate and drank and expressed their intense pleasure at being all together there—a little tribe—a long-term team—a lost army unit—a disrupted happening—a genetic pool—a cross-pollinated forest—a family. Candles dripped in the fog, their butter yellow tips slipping into jars. Billie sprawled against Tom, her hand locked between his folded thighs, warm, and at an angle so Dan could see the old tracks in her arms. She said it was intensely exciting to commit incest with someone who wasn't her brother.

Late that night Jesus came to visit Tom. He tracked him down where he stood in the motel hall outside his brother's door. Tom had just said goodnight to Dan and went to the

outer door to check the fog. He stepped out. The moon was
smoking. The fog was thinning. A fountain rolled with water
and there Tom gazed at an image which he saw rising as
from the spring of a spirit. It was hardly bigger than a bub-
ble, but it was Jesus dressed in white, with brown skin, more
modern than Tom ever imagined him, because he was so immediately recognizable with his easy attitude, and a sweet
smile on his lips. Tom felt all his desire pour into the light-
ness of the water which sustained this image, and he realized
that the water was actually light. He knew if he should reach
out and touch it, it would ripple and vanish, and so he stood
like one petrified, pouring all his desire out on the sweet-
smiling form who slowly backed into the nothingness he
came from.

Tom returned to his room, where Billie was on the phone.
She slapped it down fast. An unnatural smile twisted her lips.
Her knees were up, tenting the sheets, she threw them back
to expose her naked body as if it were a surprise, small and
neatly wrapped. He stripped, remembering how she felt, but
his heart was like a red plum floating in pain outside in the
fog while his mouth was sealed. The name Jesus was an im-
print tight on his tongue, something he wanted to swallow
and incorporate into himself.

He pressed his face into the curve of her neck, seeking ordi-
nariness, her hair on his lips and eyes, and he nearly gagged
on the emptiness he felt. It was the next thing to bliss. She
stared across, then hoisted him up. Asking, Want a little
something for the pain? He raised up:

What?

A little something, she repeated, like coke or even heroin.

But you know I don't do that anymore.

Just a tad now you're so sad? It rhymes!

I thought you didn't do it anymore either.

I don't or only on rare occasions. Like now. Come on. She rolled onto the floor and under the bed, clawing around under there as a child will do when looking for a stuffed animal. He lay flat on his back, but pulled a cover over himself, his smooth skin was covered now with goose bumps.

I remember how good it felt, it's true, he murmured, but no.

Come on, she begged from under the mattress. You know you're free of it, you've changed from those old days when Jay would deliver it to you. You're totally different. A lawyer! A man, not a boy.

He sat up then on his elbows, eyes staring at her words in the air. He leaped off the bed and fell on his knees on the floor, as if to pray, but hauled her out from under by the feet. She bumped her head and whacked him on the shoulder.

"Hey, man, why did you do that?" she screamed.

Sorry, he said, gaping at her pained expression, which was the same one she had under pleasure too. And then he decided to say nothing more, he became inwardly official, child of the law and its many doubts and amendments. If she knew about Jay, his friend and former dealer, and never said so before, everything she said was a lie and a danger to him. While her sunniness returned, swelling her face into a smile, she twined her limbs around his on the floor.

"Forget it, little brother," she said. "You don't need it. I'm sorry."

You smell like a lace cookie my mother used to bake, he told her. A lace cookie, it was called. Ha. Lace, laced? You could be laced with some ingredient which makes you as sweet as you are, and as potent, and I don't know it.

"I'm not taking anything, just wine," she murmured onto his mouth. "I told you, I'm clean."

He dragged his brother out of bed early and said they must leave at once. Billie was in a deep sleep with the pillow over her face. Dan kept hesitating and inquiring and wanting to hold back, stay longer, postpone their motions, slow down, but Tom almost brutally shoved him around. They had two cars between them, both rentals, and Dan followed Tom back up the coast highway, north around the green ravines and the cluttered chaos of Tijuana to the border.

Twelve

Meantime Money drove Felicity and the children to a flat land where she said tiles supported the surface of the earth so it wouldn't sink into the sea. Dry chaparral and avocado groves. Money gave Felicity no choice in going, but told her that Temple required her presence at once. You are, remember, his slave. Felicity was not exactly afraid but did hold tight to her children, squeezing a knee, a hand, a lump of hair, whatever she was allowed from the back seat. Then Money told Felicity about white guys who ride around in trucks, with *Soldier of Fortune* magazine and beer, and shoot at people—even at each other—randomly, for the hell of it. They hate anyone with a shadow in their skin, she said, and this includes Jews. And even Catholics, especially when they're brown. Never saw a woman among them, she added. She was snapping and popping her gum to punctuate her emotions.

Felicity meantime felt like Tom would about this story. She didn't want to know any more, but already felt sick. She hummed and curled over the seat to play with a stuffed animal. She bounced the bunny up and down on her daughter's knee, saying squeak, squeak, squeak, every bunny loves her mummy.

Temple had a bottle of Rafael and a couple of plastic glasses on the motel table when she walked in. Money took the children to a movie and Felicity, without them, felt naked. But it was Temple who was only in shorts and an open shirt. He was

staring like a blind man at the floor. Sitting in the one armchair, while she took to the edge of the bed. She poured herself a drink and waited. Cars pushed through heat outside,
one after the other, the curtains were drawn across the sun,
and the smell of green deodorizer stank up the air. There was
a black revolver on the round table. She could feel its weight
just by looking at it, as if it was an erect penis. Temple was
unaware of her, stoned, she supposed, but now she saw him
stick his thumb in his mouth, and suck like a small child,
steadily, rhythmically, an expression of docility covering his
closing eyes. Mortified at being a witness to this, and dis-
gusted at the pity it lifted in her, she lay back and dozed
across a level of nausea induced by Money and the rest. She
realized she could kill him then, there, and now. COULD,
because the gun was available and he was all but a corpse already. COULD because his insanity, she knew now, probably
didn't end in privacy, but was part of a political program.
Money didn't mention those guys in trucks for nothing. Over
politics Felicity might be able to kill, being the child of a vio-
lated history. Dozing is the poor person's meditation.

(She met God and walked with Her around the edges of a
garden. The snow had recently melted there—there were
patches of white around, and jars containing fireflies on the
planks that marked the edges of the garden. They walked
around and around a wrought iron fence, looking for access
so the old lady could sit in a safe place. When God was
seated, Felicity raised herself up on her elbows and didn't
know where she was in the world, but she yearned for her
mother, father, aunt, uncle, the snow, and her children, all
spirits who fell out of reach of her own. Temple was still
stoned, even in the garden she saw the gun, and the curve in

the back of his big nodding head, shaped like a canoe. Then he whirled around, the ground rocked, and he jumped on her, pinning her shoulders back. He accused her of spying on him, of seeing him in a moment of weakness. The mattress slipped, she struggled but all her limbs were weighted with the paralysis of her pity. Briefly she recognized the fact that it was a dream. She felt his weight across her own numb bones and wanted him to have sex with her.

Go on, she told him. But he handed her the gun, saying, Kill me, I hate the world.

The gun fell out of the motel and she chased it down the street at full speed. Her head grew into a cookhouse down in back of a plantation mansion, and there was lots of commotion around. It was in her system as it had never been before: the cookhouse, that one. She was woman to woman. They could all be mean. Even the missus was mean to the maid. She who wanted to be the ambassador of the poor, of the children, of the anonymous, of the neglected, of the injured, of the women mauled and mistreated, of the *hijos de la chingada*, of the exploited before they are ruined, corrupted and poisoned as she had been, she was now a bad one too.)

That's when she woke up on the motel floor with Temple watching her from his place in the chair and drying his thumb on his shirt.

Bad dream? he murmured.

And then he spoke: Look at me talk on t.v. I recorded it so you could see it.

Then he set the images in motion through a v.c.r. and sat smiling at himself on the screen. He was addressing a white female interviewer in a cheap studio setting.

"Hitler was a prophet, you've got to understand. Like Muhammad. Like Jesus. He had a vision. He didn't mean harm to the Jews. He simply saw the obvious. Races should not mix. Louis Farrakhan says the same thing. We agree. You stay on your side of the line. We'll stay on ours. It makes sense. This way each race develops its own abilities. Whites are the most intelligent. We should be allowed to stay clear of social chaos to pursue the life of the mind. As for all that holocaust business, no such thing ever happened. The Jews are always manipulating, interfering, they're very smart. But don't trust them. And the Papists are planning to take over the world far more than Hitler ever dreamed of. The Pope wants to rule mankind. The Catholics are confusers. They like to spawn mongrels. They talk gibberish. But they're dangerous because they lack racial principles. They want world domination the same way the Commies do. You can't school people in social etiquette in a place where violence rules. You know that, but you probably just don't dare admit it. There's a criminal ring that surrounds us all. It's like a border we don't know is there. It's the beginning of the end of all actions. You can say, Wow, those people are evil out there, meaning the execs, the corporations, the banks, the pols, the etceteras, but you're evil too because you're inside their circle, being protected by them. This is the big circle. Call it a ring. You can do wrong inside the ring. Say you know a guy who works for a corrupt boss. The boss steals, say, computer equipment from his own company. So the employee says, hey, I'm going to do that too. He gets caught and has to serve time. He is destroyed in all ways. And why? Because he thought he could play like the boss. No way. The more inside the ring you are, the more you are required to obey the laws of the power boys. The winners. To do their thing. You think I like it that way? No, I don't like it but I at least know what I know. You can't confuse things inside the ring. You gotta keep whites here, blacks there, Chicanos there, Orientals over there. I'm sure most of them would agree. Most people of all races are against integration."

The interviewer with a glazed expression turned to the camera, and smiled, with her blue silk dress wobbling against her skin, just in time for Temple to switch it off. Now he turned to Felicity with a question in his eyes. Did I look okay? I thought I looked pretty good.

Temple, if you believe all that shit, what are you doing with me? ME! she shrieked and threw loose her black hair.

Who says I believe it?

How can you go on public t.v. and say those things?

I like to see myself in lights.

I want to throw up, I don't want to live in this world any more.

Oh stop the drama. . . . Now remember who sent you to the hairy lawyer's house to stay a few months ago? When you were down and out? Remember it was a girl named Billie? She was a friend of his former dealer, our friend Jay, and they set up the living situation in Boston. Billie is one of my slaves. She was supplying the boy with drugs years ago, not that he ever got hooked for too long, but he doesn't know anything about her. He's pretty dull-witted, I guess you know. Into sex and emotion. He's down there in Ensenada right now, and she's down there working for me. Get the picture? Now I have a job for you so wipe that killer look off your face. It will entail some traveling and some danger, but not of the physical kind. I'll supply you with a car. It's about body parts, this job, not auto body parts, but ones like your little girl will be given. Kidneys, livers, hearts, that kind. You're going to be responsible for collecting and carrying them over the border. In a Playmate Cooler made by Igloo, the kind you take to the beach on a picnic with your kids. All you have to do is pick them up and deliver them to a doctor here. I have all the directions written down. It won't take long, and you're the perfect foil, traveling with two little girls and a picnic cooler.

Shit on your head. You never said this was part of the deal.

I said you were my slave.

I'm not good at slaving.

So what's left to be good at. Woman.

Moving. I want to go now.

You just take what you want and go, right?

In this case.

How do you think that makes me feel?

Like someone who did someone a favor.

I don't do favors, said Temple.

You already promised, you always keep your promises.

I don't want to have to hurt you.

Why not? Go ahead.

How do I know you and the hairy one, Esau, won't talk?

His name is Tom. You don't know.

That's right.

He has nothing to do with anything.

Look, Felicity it's just a matter of grace and attitude. I made you a promise and you made me one.

I hate you. I hope I'm there when they catch you and hang you. Rat bastard. Slime of the earth. Satan. I'll do it but don't hurt anyone but me. Get it?

That sounds slavish. I could refuse the liver to your daughter.

Come on.

Why not. That would do it.

Take my kidney instead. How's that?

Sounds good.

Take my body parts and sell them.

What'll be left?

Whatever you don't need.

I might need your heart. We're looking for one.

Okay. Take it.

It's worth about 30,000 bucks.

I'd rather live without a kidney.

Of course you would.

How much is that worth?

About 3500 as you know.

So what are you gonna do?

Take your kidney and something else.

What.

Your eyes.

Felicity rubbed her eyes. Then she said,

> Okay, but I hope you die in a fire so no one can use any
> part of you. Evil thing!

Her curse, so passionately made, disturbed him, and he
grabbed her by the arm and held her against him as they
walked outside to the car. He talked tight and quick.

I am not evil, Felicity. Believe me. You have to think realisti-
cally and not in those primitive terms. We live in a waste
economy. We produce waste. Kids who have, and kids who
don't have—they're all part of it. You're right about luck and
money, but it's an old story, a boring story. Look at the military instead. For what? It's thousands of dollars, hundreds of
thousands, each time they send out a boy to exercise a piece of
metal in the sky. The taxpayers don't bitch about that, they
bitch about poor people and prisoners. Practice for what war?
War is no longer the issue. Government is no longer the
issue. Business is. Business runs the world. Not government.
Street kids? There are drillions of them, all like living abor-
tions unwanted by anyone. I'm in the business of recycling the
organs. The lucky ones win. In this case, for once, you're one
of the lucky ones. Now, here's the address—directions—of
the place you're going to. Here's the car. Your girls are already
waiting, with the cooler on the back seat. Go on now. Just go
to the place, walk inside, they'll take the cooler, fill it up, you
turn around, and drive right back across the border the way
you came. How can that be hard? We're talking about saving
your daughter's life. This is materialism, this is it.

Blasting the radio on a jazz station, Felicity drove an old rat-
tletrap south towards the border, and paused there before
crossing over. She hesitated because she was tempted to tell
the men in uniform about Temple, about her assignment, and
the reason for the empty cooler on the seat in back. But she
couldn't bring herself to do it—for reasons as old and polluted
as the rivers which lived near people. Fish washed up belly up.
Birds teetered and keeled to the side. Their feathers blew like
dandelion fluff across the top of such a river. Lazy morality,
slow water, the motion of her own history, and its attachment, hers, to the child on the seat beside her.

So she drove on down, following the directions given to the
clinic where he wanted her to collect the organs and drive
them directly north again. Not just one. Not just the one for
Matty, but many. The girls were playing with a mix of soldiers and dolls, the soldiers being so much smaller than the
dolls that their shaven heads reached only to the unmarked
and empty female crotches waving over them. The girls had
no idea why they were making this trip, but Lee was uneasy,
squinting her eyes into razor-like slits as she glanced out at
the passing landscape.

The clinic was near a stagnant lake in a desert landscape
where a highway—or was it an airstrip—came to a halt, and
up and off in the brown hills there was this little building
with the kind of chimney she had only seen in crematoriums.
Two new cars were parked in front, and Felicity pulled up
the old Ford she had been given and stared at the building.
Lee asked what was wrong. She told her nothing. Matty said

the place reminded her of a chicken coop and went on playing. Felicity finally climbed out, telling the girls she would
only be a few minutes. Lee handed her the cooler, asking, not
for the first time, what she was picking up.

I told you, said Felicity. Something disgusting.

   Poo poo? asked Matty, grinning.

Yes. A sample of cow poo. Don't look at it when I bring it
back. It stinks.

   Who wants it? asked Lee.

Temple. And Money. They're doing an experiment.

Felicity left the car and walked to the door, but stopped
again. Her breathing was quick and dry. She felt faint. She
walked around to the back of the barracks-like structure, and
tore at her face and scalp. She made the twisting motions of a
mime performing AGONY. Beside her was a window and
she lifted herself to peer inside, one knee bowed up against
her belly, the foot on the other leg stretched to a point.
Inside she saw two corpses, half covered with sheets. Flat-
chested girls. The room's white walls seemed to bulge from
the weight of the ceiling. She saw an open door at the end of
the room, no one was there. And she saw arched brows, light
smiles, and hanks of black hair swirled back from the two
young faces. But what she focussed on was their eyelashes
dipped at the base of their long eyelids. Black lashes, longer

than any she had ever seen, perhaps because of the profundity of their repose. Each tiny hair might have been doubled by its own shadow, she figured, and that was what made them seem so long and so silky. Or maybe it was just the word "lash" for such a little thing that made them into such a strong thing? But she was stunned by the image of those drooping eyes. No longer in service to the female bodies that were only half-developed. Undeveloped. Pinocchios. Boys with girls inside. Incomplete works. Lashed down. Christ's back lashed in the stations, lashed to royal stripes, the cross lashed to his back, and the donkey following. . . .

She stumbled downwards and landed on one knee in the dust, then plunged along forwards, gasping, back to the car. Already the front door was open and a woman waiting there for her, but she ignored the cries from this woman, and banged inside the sanctuary of her car, driving off at top speed in a whorl of brown sand. The two girls clamored with questions, demands for answers, which she didn't give, but rocked instead, side to side, in the car seat, humming like a fly.

If she looked at Matty, she yelped and cried. So she didn't look at Matty. Instead she blocked out all their queries, and drove like a maniac past silver olive groves and pepper trees.

The soul is a space and cries out to Jah who is the rest of it. But the mind tries to remember what the ancestors said. Because it's all there, stuck up inside the DNA—the cells of the baby mind con-

tain and continue all history. Fragments of a united front—blocks of split text from an original Logos. I know it.

Those queer night sounds and the speed at which the stars machined their way through the sky—or was it earth moving? I never remember—were Abba's attempts at capturing me. But when G-d is a metaphor for d—th, then I cry out: Rescue me from Yahweh my enemy, and from unjust people and their decisions. Why should I care? Why has the enemy thrown me this far from home? Why is my enemy my only hiding place where I feel safe in the world?

She assumed the enlightened one would forgive her, who cast her eyes towards the earth where flowers doll up the plod through dust. And she sensed that humans are a race of elves. It made her laugh.

She wants only to get close to Alpha & Omega so there will be no more fear of the world. High fertility rates among the Latino and black communities make others hate them. Today the surf will be six feet, a green ray like lime pie on a watery table will follow the sunset. Caused by transport smog, white caterpillars finger up the Interstate.

To accept the duality of Jah is an impossibility; it is a contradiction in terms and must not enter the head of any individual. Technology's cunning turns halos into auras. It makes morbid men who only like snow-women with berries for lips. But I say that snow's white powder should knock down the high price of software and crystal.

For one thing, my loneliness was intense. It became my condition by a process of elimination made without logic or choice. She lost three pints of semen over the long run, each one was a wee child. Meanwhile my emerald did not change, but stayed as solid as a frozen ocean, a bottle chip, a chameleon on a leaf.

I lacked a community beyond my family and had but two friends with whom I could discuss sacred texts. A truant child was hidden in myself on the way to church, and a playing card with a duck painted on it, the kind you kill. I thought I'd like to be children again in an illustration, mallard-colored.

The rest of the time she labored in front of strangers. When a black hole swallows matter, it's light-years away from earth and millions of times as far away as Pluto. We're really lucky. Out of it comes a stream of X-rays and green prayers.

When I lay in blankets in the dark and empty house I heard sounds which made me cringe. Fuck you, someone shouted at a child. But on my flying carpet, I could go as high as cloud-seeding experiments in the Sierra Nevada. It was there that I felt like a surrogate mother raising the question, Who owns the individual?

Night sounds were neither animal nor technological and the stars moved abnormally fast. I felt that Abba was demanding my attention, then yearning for it (here I say "I" and "my" but always mean "human") out of its spatial isolation. Another Santa Ana was moving in, peaking air pollution, and sea swell. From Point Pinos to Point Conception, hazardous seas and escapees. The sea under the rising sun was like an oriental rug for lying and flying on.

She lives with an oppressive sense of eternity and its presence in her, and is truly impatient of people who say, "You're lucky. Your faith must make you very happy." How is she supposed to be happy with eternity? Can you tell me that? You must be crazy. What exists is named specifically, and there is no specific name for G-d. In the mountains are snow guns and enough high-tech gear to pilot a Lear jet. The wild cats leap down a hill called Sheep Dip. In lace tulle and millinery flowers stands the bride of snowmen.

I only want you to know that the bread of heaven feeds the poor human soul, begging only to be nourished in peace. Waste water is recycled into drinking water. There are lots of wonderful Americans out there whose self-hatred takes the form of rejecting immigrants. The sky is teeming with hidden blue machinery. And each act is the signature of thought, especially the sign of the cross.

I knew it was unpopular to think there was a city in the sky, one that scientists and satellites couldn't see yet, and even as I tormented myself with the idiocy of such a thought, I counted its turrets.

A command came out of the river: Mistreat the dark man, woman, and child. She felt weary and grave, a pilgrim bewitched by drugs and shades. Like a horse wearing a veil, the man at the border patrol, asking for ID's.

Everything is structured and complete. There is no physical matter that does not contain its precedent. Yet we are given lies and clamber up the facts like old hippos. At the zoo the animals are hardly more alive than photographs, yet people stand and snap pictures of these images. I think we all want to get back to the beginning to see what happened next. Physicists, as hardheaded as peanuts, want this as much as anyone. They talk about eddying water and how the ripples all come together in patterns of patterns. I've heard them. They are desperate to understand what happened first.

With a ring in his earlobe, sandy hair and red fuzz on his white upper lip, the patrolman acted like her boss. Two whites hovered over some fossils, and pink pajamas were hot and excited at the end of the motel. Oranges hung on trees and in the eyes of the orangutan was the whole world.

Down the river in rubber the alien was a kind of mud wall with eyes. Grass swayed where the hunters puffed. She spoke of the material body. Who belonged where and to whom. In Balboa Park one immigrant's mouth full of mud made her spit. She re-

membered a floating head, water full of dogs and wooden noses. Empty yourself to G–d, she said.

The earth trembles here and the orange rocks are heaved up at an angle in the deep canyons. This is a place where you can wash in the wind, but can never return to the heavy city.

My enemy is often my leader, especially when I have everything I need. He takes me where there are landmines, then, and where there is fresh water. I have less fear when my enemy is my guide because he draws me into meandering areas where I feel protected from the long shadows of evening. He comforts me. He knows where the dangers are that he himself planted. So how could I feel safer than when I am with him?

She has a terror of marriage because it takes a promise she can't keep. She really doesn't give her secrets away to many people. Like a gnome who fell from the sky in a bag and flopped around screaming on the ground, she's at the mercy of her birthweight and nothing else. The fact is, humanity has an adversarial relationship to that space which threatens the material body. In the desire to appease the wrath or appetite of this space, we develop many forms of behavior, most of them in postures of terror. We wish G–d was d—d so we could take care of our own prison.

The Saint Augustine Bingo Program and the price of cement in Mexico are linked by a convent. There they paid her to laugh and brought the price of cement down at the border every time she did. By this time the sight of a uniformed police officer was almost a comfort. Back at Pleasanton Federal Prison people wondered which of the twin cities was the most important one.

Little fishes go in and out of a net and don't even know they're all wet. Diabolus simius Dei.

Stimulate ovulation in a dragon and you need to collect semen preserved in an old kimono. But who owns the seed? Confusions mark the end of an era. However negative, it's necessary to press on.

I think airplanes need eyeglasses as much as their pilots do. Technology has run ahead of ethics. Blustery weather in San Diego Bay and northeast is a dreamscape on the berm of Sunrise Highway. Bright-colored sleds, a rolling fog. In a materialist world the body is the ultimate possession of value. You feel like someone left in a refrigerator for years. Geographics are as cozy as nurseries or weddings smothered in headpieces, tulle, favors, bouquets, corsages, and ribbons by the bolt.

At the Rosarito Beach Hotel, a blue tiled bathroom and a blue tiled pool, white wicker chairs, and the sea, and horses. They had travelled on foot over black sand with rippling lines like shells to the mountains. Olive trees and jars of condiments at roadside stands. Is desperation truer than joy? Green seahorses on the tiled floor were nearly worn away by the vomit of American marines.

If ideology can be a substitute for action, then so can questions be clues. The muff and stick were in bed pretending to be illegal aliens. So ideas suffer humiliations you never even dreamed about.

Twin dogs in matching plaid sweaters stopped in the back of a truck at the border. One ran after a bugger, another after a beggar. I didn't know which was which only that this was that.

She was working at the orphanage. Her excitement was prodigious. A bad mother sat on the beach. For her all too human cruelty I would still call her pathetic. She trailed across the sand like some alcoholic tenant at a resort. The father arrived, smaller by a fart, and like a spider, rubbed his elbows and knees together saying, My sexual energy is high. He was laughing so I laughed and got paid again. The children wondered who owned the eggs on the stoves, while they starved.

I had in my possession a band of foundlings, with round faces, brown as flan, *and the smell of chickens in their feathery skin. My joy sang in my fingertips at both the saw and the stove. I could hold, in this fifty-five inch frame, a tribe of free souls. I had forgotten though that I was south when I was and north when I was. Every bountiful place seemed to be an interval in a directionless galaxy.*

I've caused you so much trouble, darling, darkling, chica *and* chico. *Bite something rotten and you've got the essence of dreams, she told them. Do you apologize to cats when you push them off a chair? I bet you do. The borderland is no fairy place, so don't be afraid when the barns thunder with trampling and strangling, when the wooden infant grows a nose as long as Pinocchio's. I value nothing more than your voices, she continued saying. Like a flight of birds from an empty brown hood outside a little hermitage, a deluge of candles wobbles in your breath.*

Twelve little faces turned to hear her. She wanted only to take care of them, to unfold them joint by joint until they could rise each day, eyes dark with joy knowing the hand of love would return and never forget them.

That was, however, never to be her vocation. Or mine. An error on the part of my compass, or an act of predestiny? We will never know. Hands are still the physical parts which give me the most delight. Look at them some time.

I personally was given the charge of a mad man, instead of children, and a bunch of white people, of which I was part one, crawling here and there useless as mushrooms or ushers in a dark theater. I kept a dollhouse instead of a photograph in my cell, later, in order to give me a remembrance of all the mansions in eternity. D—th, of course, is the winner, since we have to pass through it to escape it. But being alive, instead of never-here, still excites me, I'm happy to say.

Thirteen

Back in the world of commerce and voice, they stopped at a border town to breathe. She had driven so fast that she herself felt defeated. Now she was pasted in an outdoor cafe, with her girls sticking on either side of her. She was watching the crowds, traffic, individuals, most of whom she didn't like, except for the children begging and playing. She kept her head averted, wouldn't look at Matty, and only flashingly at Lee. "If something bad happens, blame it on me," she told them softly.

You're scaring me, Ma, said Lee.

Don't be scared. We're fine.

But you didn't do what Temple said.

I'm not his slave.

Won't he get mad?

Probably.

Will he still fix Matty?

Oh I'll probably look somewhere else for help.

Maybe Tom can help?

He's smart, maybe he can.

What will we do with the car?

Leave it and take the bus home.

Ma, they're going to get mad.

Just try to be happy right now.

Happy?

Can't you be?

Lee looked perplexed, and troubled, thinking, but Matty threw her head back, and began to chant and jerk her knees up and down in time to her litany.

I'm happy in my bottom.

Happy on my left side.

Happy on my right side.

Happy in front of me.

Happy behind me.

Happy on my back.

Happy in my hands.

Happy under my feet.

Happy in my mouth.

Happy in my ears.

Happy on my head.

Happy in my stomach.

Happy in my spit.

Happy in my pee-pee.

Happy in my hair.

Happy nowhere!

Okay, Matty, we got your point, said Lee.

Happy in the air, the little girl added quietly.

Felicity said, I could work in an orphanage again, and we'd all be safe. We could go back to the *Ciudad de los Niños de Infantile Mariana.*

She glanced at Matty who was as yellow as a sunflower, and whose eyelids drooped in spite of all efforts at liveliness. Felicity swung away and stared into the street, her eyes burning.

I want to go back to our house, said Lee. Ma!

I do too, said her sister.

But don't you like it here? All these kids? People?

No.

No.

Life is easier here. No rush and tension. No shelters. No
competition. What do you say? We might be able to find
good medication for Matty. We might!

No.

No. I want to go home.

But why?

We want you to settle down.

Get a job.

Marry Tom.

Be normal.

A real mother.

Please.

What?

Please, Ma?

Let's go home.

A real mother?

Sensible. You know.

Stop smoking.

And drinking beer.

Clean the house.

Go to work every day.

Get me to school on time.

Me too.

Nothing much.

We love you. I do.

Sensible?

She doesn't have to be sensible.

Okay. Just normal.

Please, Ma.

If you do, then you'll be happy.

We know it.

I am happy.

You don't seem it.

You seem sad.

You're always running away.

Please, Ma.

Go to AA.

Matty uttered this instruction in a soft slurred voice. Her face was seriously jaundiced, as were her corneas, and she was slumped back in her chair with her wrist resting on a trembling hand.

Ma, Matty looks horrible.

Go on talking, said Felicity, her expression set in stone.

We love you.

You'll get sick if you don't.

Take care of yourself.

Maybe Tom loves you.

No, he doesn't. He just likes her.

Okay, but he'll be a help.

She's gotta do this alone.

Be a grown-up?

No.

What do you mean then?

She's gotta live a regular life.

That's a grown-up.

I hate grown-ups.

So what should she do?

Take care of stuff, us.

And still have fun?

She can still have her beer.

No cigarettes then.

Right, yuk.

But I doubt if she'll give them up.

Or get a job.

No, she's had jobs, she can.

Please, Ma, I promise I'll get better at home. Or if we go to the seashells, said Matty and again her voice slurred and her hand trembled.

Better? Felicity inquired. Better? You are the best. And the illness is just part of the perfect you, that's all. You're perfect. What is this "better"?

You know what she means, said Lee.

I feel better already, Matty said.

I know what she means, but I know what I mean too.

Felicity stole a look at Matty arched lightly back in a wrought iron chair. Lee stood up and stretched, saying, Let's go, you guys, in a motherly voice.

Matty climbed up on Lee's back and Felicity walked behind, holding her up with her hand. She was not conscious of her hair turning silver under the sun.

Fourteen

Tom and Dan walked along the sand which was blackish and flecked with gold. High reddish cliffs walled them. The water shoveled at itself—white and green shavings, clarities of light slipping through the shaft of a wave as it broke. The beach wound towards La Jolla, crouched in the sea like another Monte Carlo. They tiptoed over rocks and shells, watched a seal and moved on, till they came to a beach where bronzed men played badminton, jogged, lay flat, had sex, or waved to them, all naked except for hats. There they turned back. Dan did much of the talking, still walking with the halting steps of a blind person, his knees bumping, his feet crossing, his hands gesticulating.

It sounds like Felicity is a pathological liar, Tom, and you've been taken in. I mean, let me go and meet her and judge for myself. Of course if she's not lying, then you'll have to report the story to the police. Won't you?

I don't know, said Tom.

Well, why not?

I'm leaving. I want to go back home.

What's wrong with you?

Tom lifted his hands and dropped them again, and told his brother he should stay, even without him, and enjoy the fine weather. There's nothing wrong with me, he said.

She sounds like one of those people who are completely unable to learn from experience, said Dan. Know what I mean? I mean, most people have trouble with it, but she's taken it to the limit?

Experience seems very feeble to me at the moment, said Tom. Like the law, I don't find it satisfying as a way to respond to certain problems.

I could've told you that years ago, said Dan, but you wouldn't have had the experience to understand my meaning!

Tom looked up at the sky where clouds were as thin as frost on a windowpane, and remembered a visionary dream: thin jets of milk issued from Felicity's breasts and filled a row of twelve white cups. Again, the same Jesus, brown as wood, stood with her. She would lean on him and he would feel nothing. Then she asked, Milk with your tea? And sliced a hard loaf of brown bread with a silver cleaver. And now the room filled up with children who drank her milk greedily and ate her bread and she still leaned the weight of her body on Jesus who said, *To each a Lord according to her need.*

Are you in love with her, Dan asked.

With Felicity? I'm not in love with anyone.

Well, something is strange. I think you are. In love. With her.

I wouldn't leave if I was, would I, said Tom.

Yes, it's exactly what you would do.

> No, it's more that I feel like I'm caught in a tide pool—too many walls, connections, the same whirling faces again and again. Temple is probably pulling my strings, for all I know. I feel like I'm in a purgatory of people.

So I took the plane home before Felicity and the children came back again, and left Dan in my place. The transaction was, on the surface, a matter of the following: I believed she would be safer with him there, since he had no connection to any of the people involved. And I wanted him to have an extension of his vacation. He looked tired, a little shaky, ready for a break. I knew that Felicity would let him stay there with her, because it was in her nature to share what she had with anyone. I also had an instinct about the two of them—that they would connect in deep, quick ways. It would not be the first time that I gave to Dan a treasure or a secret I could have kept for myself.

Above all else, I was relieved I would not have to say goodbye to her and the children. If dying was distancing oneself from the things of the world—and the evidence of the world is conclusive on this score—then saying goodbye was too much for me to handle right then. Especially to Matty whose nervous gestures and luminous eyes would not leave my mind.

As I bounced through the clouds, the flight seemed to be a metaphor for my own helpless condition. I couldn't, and I hadn't, really helped anyone on that trip. Not even myself!

I had seen the red sea and sky melt into one horizon: the borders were as feeble and as vulnerable as my own forays into relationships. The verdict so far showed that a response was always missing from my actions. All I ever did was listen. While it made me a useful companion up to a point, in the end I could see myself becoming nothing but an anecdotal old man, someone who told other people's stories. The law bored me, before I had hardly begun my career, and the thought of day after day of paperwork, and night after night of solitude, was horrifying. It was especially horrifying because I knew I lacked the will to transform myself. I wished I could take Matty's illness into myself, and be the dying one that I really was, instead of her. I wished this with my whole heart.

But my whole heart, in those days, was only half the usual human heart. When it was full, it was only half a heartfull.

Fifteen

The story of Matty came later, in bits and pieces, there and here. Felicity and the girls arrived by buses exhausting in the dusk, the day after I left. They had bounced from one bus terminal to the nest, sat among purgatorial crowds waiting, strapped to luggage and t.v.'s and each other's hands. Homeless people hovered outside every terminal, begging, raving, sleeping. The children became increasingly sorrowful at everything they saw, but Felicity bucked up their spirits with stories about her childhood in Maine, stories which provided them with images of water and trees. They told her some stories, too. And they dozed all over each other like a family of cats. Hot and cold kept switching. Bus to air to terminal and back again. When they finally saw the shiny graph of buildings which meant the sea was coming close, they rejoiced and began grooming themselves. At the terminal they had one more ride up the coast on a regular bus to a stop near their house. They saw lights on in their house, a car. The girls thought it was Tom, but Felicity was filled with the bile of dread.

She found Dan, a stranger, listening to her radio and lying flat out on the sofa. She was wild with suspicion, but he proved his identity with a license and a picture of Tom which he carried everywhere in his wallet. So now she relaxed and the children were exuberant at being home. Felicity headed for a beer at once, and slammed around her rooms, while the girls took a long bath. Dan explained what had happened to him and Tom, telling her about Pedro too, and about

Mexico, when she asked. She guzzled her beer and stood looking down, her face suffused with varying emotions.

She put the children to bed, showered and returned to where Dan still sat, erect and formal, a bit embarrassed, on her sofa. Her hair was soaked into strings on her shoulder and back, she wore a white terrycloth robe, and her bony feet were bare. She told him she was afraid for her life, but she wanted him to go out and buy some food. She gave him a list and he left, agreeably.

At the mall he did all the shopping quickly, under a feeling of pressure he couldn't identify. He was hot and trembling in a confusion of appetites and hungers. He hurried back to the little house and together they unloaded the groceries. She asked: How long will you stay?

Can I spend the night? Then I'll leave.

Stay here!

She cooked some pasta for them with rapid, almost spastic gestures, as if she shared his deranged appetite. They sat at the card table in the kitchen, gulping down their food in silence, when they heard a car outside. Felicity almost threw up. She jumped up and rolled her children out of their beds, and made them lie down under them. She told Dan to hide in the bathroom while she went to answer the knock on the door.

A young white guy was there, carrying a suitcase. He said he was trying to raise money for his education by competing in a door-to-door sales program. If she bought his product, he would get her money plus the same amount again. It was a blue cleanser which you diluted with water. She looked past him at the rotund moon. She told him she was sorry but had no money and slammed the door in his face. Then she ran back to her children and put them in bed again. In the room behind the kitchen, she found Dan and fell against him, gasping on her own breath, as if it were an obstacle to her survival.

Let's walk around the house three times, he said.

Outside the moon was so bright, the whole world was alight. Bushes, trees, paths, houses. They could hear the cave-like roar of the ocean. The third time they came back to the front of the house, Temple was there.

Go inside, she told Dan. Watch the kids.

She walked over to where Temple stood by the side of the road, next to a glittering puddle. No cars passed. His head was nodding more than usual and he wore a smile he had not worn for years. It was almost radiant.

So, he said.

So.

Sleeping with the other brother now?

No, neither.

At least the other one is good and gone.

Correct.

Back to Boston.

You know everything, why?

You look scared.

Money said you would kill me.

Why would I do that?

For failing to be your slave.

She doesn't know me any more than you do. It's sad.

I don't know you, it's true, any more.

You still want that liver?

No. Not the way you do it. I'm going to turn you in.

That's tragic, childish. It makes me feel bad.

So what are you doing here?

To say goodbye.

What?

I'm leaving, for a long time, south, way south. To the Cape of Never Mind.

Why?

The people I work for were disturbed by the way you ran off. My fault for choosing you. But I've got to move on.

And?

I want you to do one last favor for me. Restore my reputation

What.

Stop trembling, it doesn't suit you.

What.

Marry me.

She observed the moon to be a disk behind his head; how white he was—a Moby Dick of a man. He was wearing white too, a camelia pinned to his lapel and one, in pink paper, in his hand. The collar was tight on his throat, so a slip of flesh folded over it. His head nodded up and down instead of left to right, and he seemed to be saying yes for her. No, she replied, I never, and you know it.

He smiled with the condescending radiance of an imperial figurine, a look she hadn't observed on his face for years. There's a long story behind all this, he told her, but I'll make it short. You must at least give me a chance to explain. And as he explained, he pinned the camelia on her terry cloth robe, and gently nudged her to the side of the road.

"Many years ago, two representatives from the American Civil Liberties Union tried to raise funds for some witnesses who had been summoned before the House Un-American Activities Committee. They went to a Communist Party meeting in San Diego to do this. My father was one of them. He was a paid informer for the Committee, in fact. While he was at this meeting, he was shot by the father of your friend Dan, inside your house now. That was the end of my father. I was a young boy, it was before I met even you—but it ate at me, as they say, and I stayed interested in that man, Pedro. His family. He's been in prison for many years as you know. I have been working for our government, Dear, against groups who try to subvert our democratic system. This includes the marketeers in body parts. You were included in my plan to bust them. But that's okay. You didn't. You stayed clean which is the way I always liked you anyway. . . . Do you understand? I'm not the son of Satan you have imagined me to be. I work for the Government! Now I'm being sent to Latin America, and I'm certainly not asking you to come with me. I don't even want anything to do with you. Like that. But I want you to be my wife."

Fat chance, said Felicity. He slipped away from her side and squinted down the street until a car dislodged itself from the oppression of shadows, turned on its beams, and swung up beside them. He pushed Felicity into the back seat and joined her there. The driver was the student with the cleanser for sale.

Take us on down, Preacher, said Temple. He pulled from his pocket a marriage license, already sealed, with both her and his name on it. He flashed it in front of her with his white teeth gleaming a smile.

It's done, without your consent, I know. But now you can perform the holy act of matrimony on the beach beside me. This man is a legitimate minister. He will do the honors.

Why are your teeth so white? asked Felicity.

I had them fixed—coated—this afternoon, he admitted.

Why are you pretending to be good? You know I know you.

It's not an act.

So what about my children?

Conveniently, you have someone there to watch them. I thought we'd have to bring them along, and that would have complicated matters. To put it mildly.

Felicity stared out the window at a cradle-shaped beach, black and white water tugged around by the moon above. Her eyes burned. She licked a tear from the crest of her lips. She wrung her hands and contemplated leaping from the vehicle. She palpitated in her throat and swooned. He put his hand between her legs and sighed with his head back and eyes closed. He looked so fine, anyone would believe he was a good man. He was colored so white in the night, a lot of people would think he was even a transparent man. She didn't, and at no point did she believe that he was the same one she loved before either; he was worse; he was a winner.

The man married them on the border between the United States and Mexico. Temple stood on the Mexican side of the beach, she on the U.S. side, the preacher between. She couldn't stand up for long and had to be married sitting down, in her robe, staring down at the sand as if it was a star in the sky: a phenomenon in which one could not geniunely believe. It was not just the mention of the Holy Name that sent her to the ground, but the terrible promise which she was making there and then; these were the usual wedding words and followed the ones she had sworn she would never utter (I do, I will) again and which still filled her with bile and grief. After it was over, she rolled on her side in the sand, and the young minister disappeared up the slope at the back of the beach and alongside Tijuana. Temple tapped her with his shoe, then, satisfied, followed the other up the slope and had him as his lover for the night. Felicity lay in the sand transfixed by the sky. Alone in the warm dawn she walked through a marsh to look at birds feeding. Already dune buggies with red and white American boys inside shot past them—it was Saturday—and a group of Mexican youths in American t-shirts charged into the bamboo-littered water, stripping, escaping. By now Temple had joined her and he smiled benignly at their moves; he was disheveled and rough-jawed, and said, We let a few through the border every day, referring to the Mexicans.

Again he walked away from the beach to a parking area to see what the Reverend could do for him, while she watched four women running, babies bound to the chests of two of them. They wore raggy colors, pants under skirts; their hair was in braids as black as her own. They too plunged in a bunch through the reeds glutted with hubcaps and engine parts and cans, and hit the water with lighthearted shouts. It was murky water, brown as their skin; they seemed to become fluid and formless, she witnessed four women and two infants, on the run and splashing through the sloughs. Anonymous and red-faced, they were stripping as they fled north. She cheered them on, excited by the mirrorish vision of watery women breaking into parts. Then Temple returned like something hard and white that lives without sun, and she steered him away from the sight of the women back up the hill the way he came.

Soon he returned Felicity to her home the way he had brought her—the young minister yawning at the wheel—and said he would keep in touch with her, make sure she had a roof over her head, and would send her regular support checks. He maintained his dignified and kind demeanor to the end, when she found herself standing in a mud puddle by the side of the road with a wedding band on her left hand, and her terrycloth robe scattering sand.

Inside the house Felicity woke Dan from his sleep on the couch and told him the story in a detached voice. Actually he didn't know if it was her voice that was detached, or if the sleep still folded around him was making him detached. In any case he listened with gratitude at her safe return. She had been on her knees and moved in over him, as if to reach for something under his back or the cushion. When she disappeared. sand fell on him from her hair. She smelled salty and the camelia rubbed off its pin onto his chest. She climbed on top of him and lay with her cheek against his and in a matter of seconds they were all over each other in the spirit of two who don't care what they eat, they are so hungry. She was so small, most of the time his chin was over her head, or he was hoisting her around. They rolled to the floor and continued their feast down there. *If God is wood,* she said, *then club me with it.* You, he kept repeating. Dreamtime was a tool and they used it as best they could, then lurched apart, it was his dream, Dan's dream, just another thing that never happened in the world. But when he awoke, he felt as if it had.

Guilt and embarrassment burned in his face, which he kept hidden over coffee and newspaper for a long time. It was after noon before he had the nerve to open her bedroom door to check on her. Yellow sunlight—watery and evanescent—wobbled on the white wall above the bed. They were all three together under the covers, arms thrown around each other, and heads pressed close, black hair entwined with the shady depth of sea-sponge. Their eyes were opened and he hesitated, waiting for the black pupils to rotate in his direction, for smiles to decenter their faces. But nothing of the sort occurred. Instead he noticed how weighted they were, as if their flesh was burdened with liters of water, and they were whiter too. He stepped closer, smiling, and only saw Matty smile back; but her eyes were fixed on high. The other two reached up their hands to him, Felicity pulled him down so hard he fell on the edge of the child. He saw the water of their tears had soaked the edge of the sheet. It had drenched the sides of their hair. She died in her sleep, said Felicity, last night, and I wasn't there to hold her.

Dan said he would call the police and left the room with the chill of the child's bones piercing his side.

Sixteen

None of the above ever happened. According to Tom, Felicity and the girls were involved in a complicated scam, engineered by Temple and designed to throw Dan and him off the track. He came to this conclusion after Dan described Felicity's actions that day: she made him leave before the police arrived, she didn't act very upset, but reminded him, instead, of someone who has just lost her inner bearings. She had the vacuity of an angel. The house was as dim as a tomb but she was slipping around in boy's pajamas, smoking. He recounted his departure, a rush of actions aiming for a bus, and passing the police car on his way to the bus stop by the beach. Dan swore that Matty had died, but Tom refused to believe him. He kept seeing her in parks, on the subway, at the end of a supermarket aisle, but he dared not approach too closely. He was ashamed to realize he wouldn't really recognize her outside the context of their time together. A few seasons after he returned to Boston, he was taken with a mysterious illness, a problem in the inner ear, which made him dizzy, nauseous, unable to work. He had to move in with his mother, and while she tried to sell his father's paintings, he stayed in his room day after day. A couple of the urban paintings—the ones depicting human misery in parks, and on subways—sold. But the rest—the ones that were self-consciously beautiful— were rejected. These were ferns, and Tom sat with them, face to the wall. They were as useful as a bunch of keys to a huge demolished apartment building. Very little income was available to his mother and himself, while he was ill, and she finally made plans to move into a residence for the elderly. His

company did her no good. It was clear to him that she pre-
ferred the company of her own generation by then.

One day, when his dizziness was lighter than usual, he went
for a walk in a snowstorm and realized he couldn't go on with
the life he was living. His face was fiery when he went into
his room, shut the door, entered his closet and sat in a pile of
sneakers and laces. Now he remembered Matty in full detail:
one image especially, when she stood at the edge of evening
water, bony and straight, and the water extended into the sky
beyond her. He remembered having an insight, sometime
around then, that at the moment of creation the body was
made of light, and that form was solidified atmosphere, and
that the auras around the flesh were proof of the indivisibility
of matter from air. But he couldn't remember why, or when
he had such an insight, or if it was even true, or, finally, if it
mattered either way. His closet smelled like a thrift shop.
Thrift shops smelled like churches. . . . Old wood, wet wool,
used shoes. . . . And it was this simple, sensual link that
changed the direction of his days; in the closet he made
preparations to enter a novitiate in preparation for the priest-
hood. He never turned back.

Seventeen

When Felicity left the house with Lee, she only took a knapsack containing a few toys, her four books, a change of underwear, sweaters, toothbrushes and combs. She left all of their clothes, sheets and blankets behind. Anything belonging to Matty she left behind, except for a barette that always fell out of her hair, and one yellow seashell.

She didn't speak for a week. Then she had to, when she left Lee in the orphanage where she had worked, south of the border, with the nuns. She gave them the address of her one remaining relative—an aunt way up in Maine, on the Canadian border.

If she will have her, and you want to send her, or if she wants to go . . . was how Felicity explained her wishes, giving them the paper with the Maine address on it. The nuns spoke little English but nodded their assent, with their eyes fixed on the face before them. Lee was between them, almost as tall as her mother, and crying into her sleeve.

Then Felicity began walking. She walked back over the border, and up the wide freeways, along the edges of cars and condos and malls, heading north.

I lived right up next to G-d in those days; it was as big and bristling as the Southern California hills, the rump of Tijuana, the desert and the ice blue sea all together. I talked to G-d in a watery babble for several months. It was great to watch the mystery unveil itself as fact. I had never wanted more than that.

I was a slave to kindness because it was so unpredictable. Unhappiness you know, it surrounds your hours, it moves ahead and behind you, but kindness—the kindness of people, or the kindness of events—is always a surprise.

In those days kindness took the form of food, blankets and a little floor space to sleep on—there was nothing abstract in it. I liked people who gave grudgingly the best, they turned out to be the most trustworthy and consistent, asking nothing from me in return. The ones who did it as an act of contrition or martyrdom always wanted something back from me.

For many months I hitched rides north, but only got to the edge of Colorado. I cleaned houses in a new development. Rows of pink stucco condos—all identical—clustered on the poor sore back of the earth. I cleaned laundry rooms and spas, then some people's houses while they were at work. I got the money in cash and slept with it in a canyon overlooking a highway. I liked it during the day when I could lounge in the houses, on sofas, on the edges of beds, they were all like motels, hundreds of units as they called their living spaces, the realization of socialism as much as of democracy, egalitarian cages, motelitarian resting places for the havers and doers, ideal in their anonymity, their lack of chaos.

The dollhouse-maker came alive in me, exploring these interiors, thinking of how the littlest, and the ugliest, and the most movable—the motel—had become the model for the biggest, and the most vulgar, and the most entrenched—the condominium—somebody's no-home!

I moved on, trying to avoid winters, but finally having to hitch a long-distance ride with a trucker who was claustro-phobic and needed someone to take over when she got stuck in traffic or had to cross a bridge or pass through a tunnel. She understood right off that I was on a mission, but she never asked me what it was or where I was coming from. If we talked at all, and neither of us talked much, it was only about the weather, or the diner, or the cost of something or other. Mostly we listened to music.

When she left me in New York State, south of Albany, I started walking again, this time I sludged through the January thaw, and through unnatural warm days pushing on into the middle of February. By now I was talking again, to myself, and to G-d, and laughing aloud, and imagining the torch I would swing through the air.

Eighteen

I still remember the wind in the scudding clouds and wet red twigs against yellow: a yellow hill too, and a sealed door in a stone gray shack by the river, where I ran. Solid wires were pulled against the long cemented windows. A dog ran after a duck and looked into a cubby in a rock.

I stayed in a place where patients were not allowed bats or balls. Like horse heads inside human heads, we tried to decipher each other. My madness had been discovered without much difficulty. I stayed by the inferno to the end, and until my face was burning as the face of Moses might have burned when he came down from the mountain. People looked away, even as they dragged me to the wagon and far from Temple's charred mansion. Black charcoal bricquets were all that was left of his family estate, and Halloween trees.

I'm not a piece of wood you can burn, by the way, but I am a piece of human who can make wood burn.

After that act of violence, I continued to be subject to spontaneous gestures. I know how the spirit suffers from the interference of the flesh.

It was a smelly, gaseous place with soapstone basins for our shaved heads. Skin on bone since the food was mush. Often it was tubed through a nostril into the bellies of those of us who resisted, as if to say:

"If you suffered this long, you can suffer longer." Across the northern plains it's partly cloudy, though here the bricks and two-thirds of each twig are gleaming. Patients tiptoe like fairies over spots of ice.

Temperatures will not return to normal. In this case, fat red gums and fallen arches will be your lot. Granular slopes covered by snowmaking machines yellow in the setting sun, kilowatts above red.

Accept agony's invitation to a hospital and you won't return the same.

It's like walking backwards through a storm of lines and circles in a comic strip, you try turning and your scarf goes gray.

On Christmas Day, white dots float across each closed window. Stars mean flurries, and stripes mean sleet. Hail comes from above, Sister told me, but the Lord can't get rid of it.

Speaking of ecstasy, half an hour is a long time. In this state of ravishment, a body both dies and rises fresh and new.

At the forbidden green line, you are capable of anything.

Like young girls riding wooden saddles, the pink buds bounce on leafless boughs. A violent number looks like fun, they seem to insist.

A starfish detonation in the heavens, ground stations and aircraft go on alert, people shudder and hide. A polar electrojet casts a shadow over the land like a little plaid pantsuit.

Whatever you know, know freely. It's hard to express afternoons as well as vacuum cleaners do.

What would have happened to a slave like me before technology? My parents' depression was sucked in and swallowed. While they were proud, they were never demeaning of me. Fixated onto my father and staying alive, I tried to avoid violation with all the intensity of one tramping.

In my dream boots I dreamed of a sensuous Puss in Boots, lounging under a tree. But all I saw was fluid and aerobatic figures blooming in the clear night sky; they were me, they were SHE. Weak, long rays grew like whiskers out of my flesh. I loved to be alone because then I didn't exist.

My aunt the philosopher asked questions like: What is more important—a diamond, or an almond?

Between shots of medication, I confessed I would rather have a dogsled carry me to the cold than sleep all day. On those times the heavens sit on my thick head and between myself and G-d there is something like cotton in snowballs; they tell me it's the shot but I prefer to pretend it's angel hair.

Only Santa Claus, like a librarian, turned everything red and color-coordinated. In red and green. Grown-ups were buildings with apartments and staircases running up and down inside of them. I used to call my littlest child The Good Finder. Now I can never find her again, because she isn't here to hunt for herself.

Depression is a sunset emotion which comes with the regularity of the color orange. While US airplanes headed for Hanoi, we were eating lamb chops beside a highway in Mount Desert. I remember the day, and the Bay of Pigs. It's like sleeping with a loaded gun under your pillow and you dream of some dim war enacted in a snowstorm.

In hell you are forbidden work, so you can't even buy the food you want. Resistance takes the form of starvation, and then of a face averted, then of religion.

Despair and increased medication do damage to each femur and larynx.

Skeletons strain against their ropes of arteries.

My pulse was my weakest act of protest . . . about as effective as water wearing down rock.

Where are the joys, and what, my aunt had once asked me, and her answers followed:

children around a table, fresh fruit, women, a glimpse into well-known eyes, the eucharist, fishing in winter, music, a smoke, a lake.

Clean up the inpatient beds and you will soon see hills of misery growing again in each one.

I remember one veteran of pain. You'd need three doctors for that patient. They cleaned out the inside of his eyes and rolled his body away. I was proud of his determination. He found the inside out escape.

A charred black house on a windy hill. . . .

Shadows lashing its roof, the shadows of branches battling the invisible rushes, clouds gaping open, and in the air the smell of the sea—all for Satan to roam and ramble now. I am glad my friend the veteran will never have to go there, will never have to travel on the other side of the high walls.

Now I tell myself, Take a quarter hour for prayer, then return to active life over and over again repeating this system.

The body must serve the spirit, obediently, though not slavishly. The body must be dignified and always at liberty. Outside the body there is no room for tyranny.

Growing old is growing wild. Going mad is growing old too fast.

The doctor's ashes fell into a plastic bowl of warm milk. He didn't notice. Everyone had bat's teeth, and a white dollop of spittle on a lip, and flat bare feet that smacked on stone.

What's brown on a wall? Humpty's dump.

Even when we laughed, the sounds in that place were all trucklike and flushing. No birds, but high walls and a watchtower. Whenever someone called Jesus there was a blur in the air, a cloud from a thicket of clichés, and in came a church man with unguents and golden toys in his hands.

Veterans of war, of school, of family, veterans of neighborhoods, hospitals, accidents and prisons, veterans of the power bloc, and of the weak bloc, of food, hell and water, this is your conscience, a tapestry of shadows, a screen on which the shades of the living live again, trapped, without sensation. Put your knife to the grindstone, stupid.

Put your shoulder to the wheel, fool. (My chocolate milk was stuck to the bottom of my cup.) I wanted to be free of these objects. One day fifteen sweater people drowned off the coast of Newfoundland, and there was a Palm Sunday massacre farther south. A week later I heard about a man who drove a truck into a cafe and shot as many women as he could. The forbidden green line rippled in the water like a crease in marble. Auroral substorms were said to be the cause of fluorescence in the altitudes.

Let those who dare, go free, said the physician who hauled up dismembered weeds and made the water clear. No illusions ever came from one patient who commented, "We will never however be loved again as long as we are still in hell, free or not. Change our history, if you can, Doctor." Or save us, I suggested, instead.

Nineteen

One day Felicity saw her aunt. She was the size of a black-bird from where Felicity was standing. She was way out at the center of a frozen lake, fishing into a hole, and balanced on a red steel office stool. Felicity stared for a long time because the sky as was yellow as parchment ready to spill the alphabet of its snow. The ice was perilous, gleaming. Timorous, she began to walk on it. One foot after the other, her long black coat crowlike as it winged off her tiny frame. She dotted the icecap with her boot-toes, inch by inch; the ice creaked or moaned; flakes began to fall. Her eyes simultaneously stung and watered. She was terrified of expanse.

The particulars of the materials around her feet engaged and held her full attention. If she could focus on the fatty white ice, its knots and gnarls, pebbles and stuck leaves, she would be okay. My aunt loves me, she loves me, she litanized about the old lady she hadn't seen much of.

Her aunt sensed the ice rejecting another weight, turned, and, under her blue cap, blinked an acknowledgement that Felicity couldn't see. Beside the red stool was a bucket of cold water on one side, and a bucket of fire on the other. Between her two feet was a bottle of Southern Comfort. The closer these details came to Felicity, the more daring she became, and now, hurrying, she lifted her eyes up into the whiteness, and saw the snow was falling in larger flakes and faster. Not so far away, she could see the thin flying figure of a young girl skating towards her. A green cap was pulled almost over the child's eyes, her lips were pouring streamers of steam, she was smiling so enthusiastically. It was Lee. She whirred over the ruts and bumps gracefully—in tights and a ski jacket—towards her mother who opened her arms to her. And they both sank down on the ice beside the old lady. The black water rocked inside the ring of ice, where the fishing line hung loose.

The old lady lit a cigarette and handed it to Felicity, followed by the bottle of alcohol for a swig freely offered.

That's how we do it down here, she said to Felicity.

Felicity's shoulders loosened, she rested in Lee's arms, her cheeks flushing from the heat and the snow. She looked at her aunt intently, saying, I know what you mean. But the bewilderment in her eyes lasted far longer than the sound of her words, rushing through the winter air.

FANNY HOWE

Born in Buffalo, New York, Fanny Howe grew up in Boston. Her mother, Mary Manning, was a playwright and actress with the Abbey Theater of Dublin, and in Cambridge was the founder of the Poets' Theater. Her father, Mark De Wolfe Howe, was Professor of Law at Harvard University and a civil rights activist. Her sisters are artist Helen Howe and noted poet, Susan Howe.

Growing up in this lively home, Howe nonetheless from childhood rebelled, getting "kicked out" of the Buckingham School and attending Stanford University "just long enough not to get a B.A." For several years she moved around California and New York, working as a bookkeeper, clerk, hatcheck girl, and political activist.

Yet like her other family members, Howe also turned to writing, receiving national acclaim at an early age for her stories in *Forty Whacks,* for her poetry in *Eggs,* and for two books of fiction, *First Marriage* and *Brontë Wilde.* During these years she was a Fellow at Radcliffe and taught writing and literature at Columbia University and the Massachusetts Institute of Technology. While raising her three children, Annlucien, Danzy, and Maceo, she found time to publish two other fictions, *Holy Smoke* (1984) and *In the Middle of Nowhere* (1987), and several books of poetry, including *Introduction to the World, Poem from a Single Pallet, Lives of a Spirit,* and *The Vineyard.*

In the years since she became Professor of Literature at the University of California-San Diego, Howe has published two books of fiction, *The Deep North* (which *The Village Voice* chose as one of the outstanding books of 1989) and *Famous Questions*, besides writing *Saving History*. She is also a noted writer of young adult books and is currently working on video films.

Since she works in several genres, there has been no simple way to characterize Howe's work. In a North American literary world that requires such characterization, she has remained elusive. But one can recognize in all her writing a struggle between oppositions, between—on the thematic level—the sexes, social classes, races, and the internal and external selves. On a formal level these same oppositions often reveal themselves at a point where radical approaches to language and structure are played out against more normative patterns of realist narrative. Yet for all these polarities, Howe is a catholic writer who recognizes the connection between the concrete act and its spiritual reverberations, between physics and metaphysics.

SUN & MOON CLASSICS

Sun & Moon Classics is a publicly supported nonprofit program to publish new editions and translations of republications of outstanding world literature of the late nineteenth and twentieth centuries. Organized by The Contemporary Arts Educational Project, Inc., a non-profit corporation, and published by its program, Sun & Moon Press, the series is made possible, in part, by grants and individual contributions.

This book was made possible, in part, through a matching grant from the California Arts Council, the Cultural Affairs Department of the City of Los Angeles, through a grant from the Andrew W. Mellon Foundation and through contributions from the following individuals.

Charles Altieri (Seattle, Washington)
John Arden (Galway, Ireland)
Dennis Barone (West Hartford, Connecticut)
Jonathan Baumbach (Brooklyn, New York)
Steve Benson (Berkeley, California)
Sherry Bernstein (New York, New York)
Fielding Dawson (New York, New York)
Robert Crosson (Los Angeles, California)
Tina Darragh and P. Inman (Greenbelt, Maryland)
Christopher Dewdney (Toronto, Canada)
Philip Dunne (Malibu, California)
George Economou (Norman, Oklahoma)
Elaine Equi and Jerome Sala (New York, New York)
Lawrence Ferlinghetti (San Francisco, California)
Richard Foreman (New York, New York)
Howard N. Fox (Los Angeles, California)
Jerry Fox (Aventura, Florida)
In Memoriam: Rose Fox
Melvyn Freilicher (San Diego, California)
Peter Glassgold (Brooklyn, New York)

Perla and Amiram V. Karney (Bel Air, California)
Fred Haines (Los Angeles, California)
Fanny Howe (La Jolla, California)
Harold Jaffe (San Diego, California)
Ira S. Jaffe (Albuquerque, New Mexico)
Alex Katz (New York, New York)
Norman Lavers (Jonesboro, Arkansas)
Herbert Lust (Greenwich, Connecticut)
Norman MacAffee (New York, New York)
Rosemary Macchiavelli (Washington, D.C.)
In Memoriam: John Mandanis
Maggie O'Sullivan (Hebden Bridge, England)
Rochelle Owens (Norman, Oklahoma)
Marjorie and Joseph Perloff (Pacific Palisades, California)
David Reed (New York, New York)
Ishmael Reed (Oakland, California)
Janet Rodney (Santa Fe, New Mexico)
Dr. Marvin and Ruth Sackner (Miami Beach, Florida)
Floyd Salas (Berkeley, California)
Tom Savage (New York, New York)
Leslie Scalapino (Oakland, California)
Aaron Shurin (San Francisco, California)
Charles Simic (Strafford, New Hampshire)
Gilbert Sorrentino (Stanford, Connecticut)
Catharine R. Stimpson (Staten Island, New York)
John Taggart (Newburg, Pennsylvania)
Nathaniel Tarn (Tesque, New Mexico)
Fiona Templeton (New York, New York)
Mitch Tuchman (Los Angeles, California)
Anne Walter (Carnac, France)
Arnold Wesker (Hay on Wye, England)

If you would like to be a contributor to this series, please send your tax-deductible contribution to the Contemporary

1. MRS. REYNOLDS, by Gertrude Stein
2. SMOKE AND OTHER EARLY STORIES, by Djuna Barnes
3. THE FLAXFIELD, by Stijn Streuvels translated from the Dutch by André Lefevere and Peter Glassgold; with an introduction by the translators
4. PRINCE ISHMAEL, by Marianne Hauser
5. NEW YORK, by Djuna Barnes edited with commentary by Alyce Barry; with a foreword by Douglas Messerli
6. DREAM STORY, by Arthur Schnitzler translated from the German by Otto P. Schinnerer
7. THE EUROPE OF TRUSTS, by Susan Howe with an introduction by the author
8. TENDER BUTTONS, by Gertrude Stein
9. DESCRIPTION, by Arkadji Dragomoschenko translated from the Russian by Lyn Hejinian and Elena Balashova; with an introduction by Michael Molnar
10. SELECTED POEMS: 1963-1973, by David Antin with a foreword by the author
11. MY LIFE, by Lyn Hejinian
12. LET'S MURDER THE MOONSHINE: SELECTED WRITINGS, by F.T. Marinetti
13. THE DEMONS, by Heimito von Doderer (2 volumes)translated from the German by Richard and Clara Winston
14. ROUGH TRADES, by Charles Bernstein
15. THE DEEP NORTH, by Fanny Howe
16. THE ICE PALACE, by Tarjei Vesaas translated from the Norwegian by Elizabeth Rokkan
17. PIECES O' SIX, by Jackson Mac Low with a preface by the author; and computer video- graphics by Anne Tardos
18. 43 FICTIONS, by Steve Katz

19. CHILDISH THINGS, by Valery Larbaud translated from the French by Catherine Wald
20. THE SECRET SERVICE, by Wendy Walker
21. THE CELL, by Lyn Hejinian
22. ETERNAL SECTIONS, by Tom Raworth
23. DARK RIDE AND OTHER PLAYS, by Len Jenkin
24. NUMBERS AND TEMPERS: POEMS 1966-1986, by Ray DiPalma
25. AS A MAN GROWS OLDER, by Italo Svevo
26. EARTHLIGHT, by André Breton
27. SAVING HISTORY, by Fanny Howe